RESISTANCE ON ICE

RESISTANCE ON ICE

BOYS OF WINTER #2

S.R. GREY

This is a work of fiction. Names, characters, places, and incidents are products of the author's imagination or are used fictitiously and are not considered to be real. Any resemblance to actual events, locales, organizations, or persons, living or dead, is entirely coincidental.

Resistance on Ice (Boys of Winter #2)
Copyright © 2017 by S.R. Grey

ISBN-10: 0-9979749-3-1
ISBN-13: 978-0-9979749-3-5

Editing: Hot Tree Editing
Cover Photographer: CJC Photography
Model: Adrian Gomez
Cover Design: Najla Qamber
Interior Design and Formatting: by:
www.emtippettsbookdesigns.com

OTHER BOOKS BY
S.R. GREY

Boys of Winter series
Destiny on Ice
Resistance on Ice

Judge Me Not series
I Stand Before You
Never Doubt Me
Just Let Me Love You
The After of Us

Inevitability duology
Inevitable Detour
Inevitable Circumstances

Promises series
Tomorrow's Lies
Today's Promises

A Harbour Falls Mystery trilogy
Harbour Falls
Willow Point
Wickingham Way

Laid Bare novella series
Exposed: Laid Bare 1
Unveiled: Laid Bare 2
Spellbound: Laid Bare 3
Sacrifice: Laid Bare 4

SHOCK JOCK ITCH

NOLAN

"**H**ere with us on the air this morning—and it's a hot one out there today, folks—we have with us the man the *Toronto Sun* recently named 'Player to Watch This Upcoming Hockey Season.' You know him as the talented first line right winger for the Las Vegas Wolves. That's right, gang, I'm talking about the *Wolves*, the hockey team that surprised us all in June when they won Lord Stanley's Cup. So, without further ado, please join me in welcoming Mr. Nolan Solvenson."

Radio host Marty Quick turns to me and smiles his trademark cocky, wolfish grin. Damn, this guy may look like a science nerd, what with the bad comb-over and retro horn-rimmed glasses, but he has me beat when it comes to attitude.

Then again, maybe not, since swagger is my middle name.

"Hey, man," he begins, with false sincerity. "Thanks for taking time out of your busy schedule to hang with us this morning. Big congratulations on all your recent successes."

He's being nice enough, but I don't trust him one bit. Everyone knows Marty has a knack for digging up skeletons from your past. And Lord knows mine is a veritable graveyard.

I take a quick swig of the dark roast I picked up from Timmy's on my way here. It was an attempt to fortify myself for this syndicated sports talk radio interview I've resisted all summer. Sadly, even the Tim Horton's coffee I love tastes bitter today.

Forcing a smile, I reply, "Thanks, Marty. I'm happy to be here."

Am I really happy to be here?

Fuck, no!

What kind of crazy fool would purposely place themselves in the line of fire of Canada's own Howard Stern-like shock jock?

Not me.

But my agent insisted. Only because he has no idea of the secrets I have buried. Some are from my distant past, but a few are fairly recent.

One of the not-too-long-ago indiscretions involves the soon-to-be sister-in-law of Brent Oliver, who just happens to be the captain of our team. He would *not* be happy to learn I spent this past winter hooking up with his fiancée's sister. It could be worse, though. Aubrey, Brent's feisty fiancée, might outright kill me if she ever finds out I thoroughly corrupted her sister, Lainey Shelburne.

Okay, Aubrey may not *kill me* kill me, but she'd definitely crush my balls. I wince at the graphic image that conjures up, and Marty Quick eyes me curiously.

The wheels in his head are turning. He suspects I have something to hide. And I do, a lot of things, but I'm not about to share a single one with him.

We break for a commercial and, worried he'll pursue a line of questioning that could land me in hot water when we get back on the air, I try to divert his attention by wincing again. Only this time I make a big show of it, twisting around and stretching my leg out under the table.

"Fucking groin pulls," I mutter, acting all in-pain. "They're a real bitch when you sit for too long."

I don't *really* have a groin pull, nor have I sat for all that long, but ole Marty buys it hook, line, and sinker. We talk about injuries throughout the rest of the break, and when the interview resumes I bring up my summer travels as another good way to keep him off my dick.

"Sounds like you got around a hell of a lot," he says when I review, in great detail, all the places I traveled to during the off-season.

"Yeah, yeah, I did," I confirm.

The more I talk of my international travels, the more I realize this topic isn't such a great idea either. It reminds me of the *reason* why I traveled so much, and that puts me in a solemn mood. Hell, Marty doesn't need another reason to eye me up suspiciously. 'Cause then will come the questions.

Only I need to know my original plan was to spend as much time with Lainey as I could this summer. That plan was shot all to hell, though, when we went our separate ways. That's why I took up traveling the globe.

C'est la vie.

Marty does look at me a little funny when I sigh, but thankfully he just moves on to questions about our Cup run. Since these are easy ones that I've answered a hundred times, I go straight to autopilot. That gives me the chance to mull over how I should've stayed the hell away from Lainey Shelburne in the first place. Though I have to say the cards were stacked against me from day one.

Did I ever really have a chance?

Probably not, since Lainey is simply too gorgeous for any man, including me, to pass by. She's a raven-haired beauty, with the most stunning turquoise eyes, the kind a guy can lose himself in, which I did regularly. And don't even get me started on her curvy little bod.

Yeah, I was a goner from the start.

I also discovered early on that Lainey's—and I really love this one—a freak in the sack. She may very well be the most insatiable girl I've ever had the pleasure of knowing.

And trust me, I've *known* a lot.

I used to think I was high up on the freaky scale, but Lainey's right there with me. Not only does she want sex all the time, any place and any way, but like me, she's into toys and other assorted kink.

In other words, she's my kind of girl.

Too bad we couldn't make it work.

Before the bad shit went down, she and I were not only set to spend the summer together, we were also planning to meet up at Brent and Aubrey's lakehouse in Minnesota. Everything got all blown to hell when I acted like an ass.

Fuck, though, that was then and this is now.

I realize right in that moment, in the middle of this stupid interview, and while answering another playoff run question, that I want Lainey back.

Yes, I do. And I'm going to make it happen, damn it.

Marty finishes up with his Stanley Cup questions, and goes straight to the place that had me dreading this interview in the first place.

"Let's get to the good stuff, Solvenson," he begins, grinning over at me like a perv. "Word on the street is you're quite the ladies' man."

Looking down at the tiny table that separates me from the host in what has taken on the feel of a far too enclosed space, I run my hand through my dark hair. "I don't know about that," I reply. "Rumors are usually just that—rumors."

He's unconvinced, I can tell, but too bad. This is a question I plan to evade like my reputation depends on it. And it may. After I fucked things up with Lainey back in April, I was so distraught that I sought out solace in the form of a slew of strippers.

And I don't mean I found comfort in being with a new one night after night.

Er, though I may have done some of that too.

"Aw, come on," Marty continues in his patented taunting tone. "All of Canada—no, wait, all of North America wants an answer." *Shit, this show does have a far reach.* "Is it true you banged ten strippers in one night?"

I laugh nervously. "No, no, that's not true at all."

It was actually nine and occurred over the course of two days, but who's counting?

Not me. And not anyone else if I have anything to say about it. Besides, the only thing that matters is I'm not technically lying.

See, that's my shtick in life—being clever, outwitting everyone. I'm a wise old sage at the age of twenty-six. My teammates call me things like "sensei" and "Yoda." And, hey, I'm cool with that. Why wouldn't I be? It works out great for me.

That's why if I stick to the gray areas now with Marty, I can successfully evade giving him a straight answer for the next ten minutes, the time left in the interview.

Yeah, you're real clever all right. So clever you outwitted your own damn self with the shit you pulled with Lainey.

"You look a little uneasy there," Shock Jock observes when he sees me frowning. "You sure there's not even a modicum of truth to that stripper story."

"Yep, I'm sure," I snap.

I need to get out of here, and fast. I'm done talking about strippers. And I'm done with this shitty interview. But most of all, I'm done with staying away from Lainey. It's time we have a talk—a *real* talk.

And if talking doesn't work, I'll do what I do best—fuck her till she agrees to start seeing me again.

2

SERIOUSLY, NOLAN, STRIPPERS?

LAINEY

I swear Nolan Solvenson is every bad hockey cliché come to life. He's not only a manwhore; he's a manwhore who seems to have an obsession with strippers.

Nolan also has a huge commitment problem, which I oh-so-happily—not!—discovered this past spring.

And that's where I draw the line.

I could have dealt with the not-keeping-his-dick-in-his-pants issue. Simply because when he was with me *I* was the one he was taking it out for. His man-whoring started and ended with me.

And I thoroughly enjoyed every minute of it.

For all of Nolan's flaws—and yes, there are many—I can honestly say he's faithful to the core *when* he truly cares about someone. And he truly cared about me. Of that, I have no doubt. It's just that his stupid issues got in the way.

I sigh and press my foot down harder on the brake. It's a pointless exercise since I'm already stopped in traffic. But now I'm stressed to the max too.

Too much Nolan-obsessing has this effect, which begs the question—why do my thoughts still wander to that man? We're over, we're done. But it's like my heart doesn't know, particularly when I have too much time on my hands. Like now.

But oh, how've I've tried to keep extra busy this summer. I spent a ton of time hanging out with my friends, when I was still in Pennsylvania and staying with my parents. But then I ended up here in Vegas a couple of weeks ago. After having no luck back east in the job search quest, I decided to try to find a good marketing job out here.

While I search, I'm living with my sister, Aubrey, and her fiancé, Brent. Aubrey's been good at keeping me busy, but I'm kind of tiring of our endless lunches and spa dates. I'm also officially sick of helping her plan her wedding. It makes me think of Nolan…and what could've been.

I sigh. *If I were working I wouldn't have time to obsess over Nolan Solvenson.* But then again, at this point, nothing short of a lobotomy could get him out of my head.

If only he'd had the balls to move forward, I wouldn't have this problem. But noooo, that stubborn man couldn't get onboard with making any kind of freaking commitment to the woman—me!—he was doing it with regularly.

It wasn't like I was being unreasonable, either. I never gunned for a proposal of marriage, or anything as over the top as that. I didn't even rally for him to proclaim his hopeless devotion to me, though I wouldn't have complained if he had.

But truly, I really only wanted one thing, maybe two—for him to declare us as exclusive and let the world know we were more than fuck buddies.

You'd have thought from his reaction that I'd asked him to make me his wife right then and there, that night I brought it up. What with the way he clammed up and brushed me off. Too bad he couldn't have been more wrong. As established, I'm perfectly happy leaving all the annoying wedding crap to the girls who love it, like Aubrey. It seems it can take you over, and Bridezilla I'm not.

Not that Aubrey is either, but I swear ever since Brent proposed to her she's been obsessed with searching for the perfect wedding venue, scouting for the best photographer, and studying floral arrangements like world peace depends on it. Name any kind of planning-a-wedding activity, and I can assure you Aubrey's either on it, in it, or surrounded by it.

And the damn wedding isn't even till next summer, so go figure.

Me, I'm a much simpler girl. That's why when I hooked up with Nolan on New Year's Eve, the fateful night this all began, nothing about us was ever complicated. I was just a horny girl looking for a good fuck. And I got exactly that with him. See, Nolan is a freaking god when it comes to all things sex.

The things that man can do with his fingers, his mouth, his cock…

Go ahead and color me slutty, but the moment I laid eyes on him I knew he'd be good. What with the way he moved in his finely tailored dark suit, like a sophisticated secret agent on the prowl, and a gorgeous one at that. I remember every detail about him too—the way his jet-black hair was all slicked back and how his ice-blue eyes penetrated my every pore. I wanted him to penetrate something else, using his hard hockey player's bod like I suspected he could.

And he did.

Nolan ended up exploring and exploiting every secret place that night. He fucked me on his bed, on the floor, across his huge wooden dresser, and against the wall in his bedroom.

The following morning, after I left his house, which happens to be a few doors down from Brent and Aubrey's place, I felt like a woman who'd *finally* met her match.

Nolan had left me exposed, open, and wanting more. But only from him, this man who was as insatiable as me.

What woman doesn't love that quality, especially when the Mr. Insatiable in question is highly skilled?

I squirm in my seat, just thinking about it. God, I hate that he has this kind of power over me, even after not seeing him for four long months.

"Calm down," I hiss, willing my traitorous body to chill.

I haven't had sex in so long that I must be going crazy. And now I'm horny as hell. *Damn Nolan.* I swear, if I wasn't stuck in barely moving traffic, smack dab in the middle of the freaking Las Vegas Strip—and oh yeah, on my way to grab lunch *again* with Aubrey—I'd pull over and touch myself till I got off.

Oh, how Nolan loved watching me do that, among other things.

Enough! I grip the steering wheel like I used to grip his cock.

Wait, that's not helping.

I try another tactic, appealing to the one part of me that Nolan neglected—my heart.

"Yeah! He treated you like crap in the end, which means he doesn't deserve your thoughts…or your passion."

There, almost working.

Traffic comes to a complete stop, so I squeeze my eyes shut and push away any lingering thoughts of stupid Nolan.

Still not quite there, but close.

I try shaking my head like a maniac, which gives me one hell of a head rush, but does in fact dispel the last vestiges of Nolan.

Ahh, finally!

When I open my eyes, I realize I've just made a complete spectacle of myself. Great. Drivers on either side of me are peering over, brows furrowed, like they might be thinking something along the lines of, *what's this chick on and can I get some of it?*

"Hey, I'm not a druggie, people," I say, turning left and right, addressing the drivers and hoping they can read lips.

It's not entirely true, though, seeing as I'm clearly addicted to something...or, er, someone—Nolan, the sex god.

Ugh, and now I'm thinking about him again. Will it ever end?

I hope so, since showing up to meet my sister a frustrated sexual mess is not a good idea. I clearly need some kind of a distraction. Like music, or even talk radio. Wait, isn't there a sports radio channel?

I fidget with the stereo system, find a satellite radio channel—*I think that's the right one*—and crank up the volume.

But then things get worse. "No, no, not him," I cry out. "I just can't get away."

Yeah, you guessed it, the man I've been obsessing over just happens to be a guest on the talk show I tuned in.

And the world continues to conspire against me.

Sometimes when you can no longer fight, you just have to give in.

So I do.

I turn the volume even louder, filling the inside of the car with the smooth, low timbre voice of the man who broke my heart. He's saying something about rumors being just that—rumors.

Hmmm...

Marty Quick then says, "Aw, come on. All of Canada—no, wait, all of North America wants an answer. Is it true you banged ten strippers in one night?"

Whaaat? I almost plow into the car in front on me. Good thing we're moving at a crawl.

While I commence cursing out Nolan, I hear him reply, "No, no, that's not true at all."

"You better say no, buddy," I grind out, not believing him at all.

Nolan goes on to deny the story, but there's something in his tone that tells me he's lying.

"You—you *prick!*" I scream, causing the driver next to me, a sweet old grandma-type, to glare over at me and *tsk*.

Shrugging, I point down to the gear shift. "Manual transmission," I mouth. And then, since her window is down, I yell over, "I was saying *stick*, not the bad word."

Grandma closes her window so quickly I hear it snap shut. She shakes her head and makes the sign of the cross, probably condemning the possessed girl next to her—me—to hell.

Well, don't worry, Grandma. I'm already there.

The image of the man who broke my heart getting it on with ten strippers has my blood boiling. And one thing's for sure—when I do happen to see Nolan, who's rushing to wrap up the interview, I don't care if we're not together. I'm totally kicking him in the junk.

CHANGE OF PLANS

NOLAN

'm all set to work things out with Lainey. But then I realize I better know ahead of time what I'm going to say. Otherwise, with Lainey's temper, I could end up making things worse.

"Could it get any worse?" I ask out loud.

Since I don't really have an answer, and talking to oneself is a little cray-cray, I shut the hell up and resume pacing the hardwood floor of my living room.

After the radio interview, the one where Marty Quick tried to trip me up on the stripper story—like *that* was going to happen—I returned to my lonely-as-fuck downtown condo, where I'm currently trying to come up with the perfect words to say to Lainey, words that'll heal and make her forgive me. Oh, and get her back in my bed.

I may be a man with a mission, but the important thing is I am still a *man*. It's about time I remember that.

"Fuck it," I declare. "I'm done with this worrying-what-to-say shit."

Flopping down on the sofa, I grab my laptop off a side table. "I simply need to *show* Lainey how I feel. We work better that way. We're action, not words, kind of people."

It's true. Lainey and I thrive on action. So what if it's action that mostly centers on sex? It's still action, eh? I prefer to communicate with my body, anyway.

So where to start...

I need a destination.

Lainey's parents live north of Pittsburgh, in a little town called Butler. I suspect that's where I'll find her. She graduated from the University of Minnesota this spring, but here it is late August and she still hasn't found a job—a tidbit Brent let slip a couple of weeks ago when we were talking on the phone. So if Lainey followed through on what she told me she'd do if she couldn't find a career-track job by summer, she's definitely at her folks' place.

I pause, fingers hovering over the keyboard, as it hits me that I'm profoundly saddened by how things worked out.

"Yeah, that's why you're fixing it now," I mutter as I hastily type in *flights to Pittsburgh.*

The screen populates with dozens of choices, along with a straggler pop-up alerting me that a new video clip has been uploaded to my go-to porn site.

I hesitate, but then move to close out the alert, since, let's face it, I don't have time to jerk off when there's planning to do.

But then—oops!—I accidentally hit the arrow on the clip, instead of the *x*. The video starts playing and I watch for a few seconds, because hello, it's porn!

There's a close-up of bouncing boobs, and then a long shot of a rocking car. Finally, a penetration shot. I'm pretty much hard as steel now, but I close the clip, because no time, remember?

That little bit is still more than enough to remind me of my last encounter with Lainey. Just like in the video clip, we engaged in a quickie in the back of a vehicle. Our encounter occurred on a bus, though, not a car. The Wolves had just played a late-season game against the Minnesota Wild, and the bus in question was waiting to transport the team to the airport.

I knew it'd be empty for a while, and unattended.

With wicked thoughts already at play, I rushed around that night, making sure I showered and dressed before any of the other players. That allowed me time to slip out of the visiting team's locker room and call Lainey.

She was still in school at the time, but the campus was only minutes away. "Are you up for some fun?" I asked the second she answered.

"Nolan?"

For some crazy reason, I was overcome with jealousy. "Were you expecting someone else to be calling, asking if you wanted to have *some fun*?" I groused.

"No," she replied.

I breathed a sigh of relief and dialed it back a notch.

"Did you catch any of the game tonight?" I asked in a sweet tone.

"No, but I heard you guys lost."

Burn. My little hellcat was pissed I'd snapped at her. It had been a dick move, and I needed to make it up to her somehow. Good thing I knew how.

"What do you think about sneaking away and meeting up with me before the team flies out?"

"What? When? Now?"

"Yes."

"I don't know, Nolan…"

"Oh, come on. Please say yes. I need you tonight, and you *know* I'll make it worth your while."

In her snottiest-snot voice, she replied, "Hmm, I'm kind of busy studying."

Tease. She was playing hard to get. And the crazy thing was I fucking loved it. But enough was enough.

"Just meet me at the arena."

She acted bored as she replied, "I guess I could use a break from the books."

"You think, eh?" I had her now. I laughed and gave her directions. "The bus is just down the parking ramp near Gate B."

"Oh, okay." Still acting bored, she asked, "And just what are we going to do once I'm there?"

Ah, Lainey loves dirty talk and here was my opening.

"I'm going to start by fucking you hard and fast. Hopefully, we'll be done before the team files in. But if not, maybe I'll not stop, and we'll give them a show." I wasn't serious about the last, but I knew the idea of it would turn her on, my little wannabe exhibitionist.

Groaning, she replied, "I'll be there in ten minutes."

"Can you make it five?"

"I can try."

She was there in four. And I kept my promise of making it worth her while—using my mouth—before anything else happened. When the rest of the fun started, I don't know if it was because we were still keeping it a secret that we'd been hooking up since New Year's, or maybe it was just the possibility of getting caught while fucking in the bus, but in any case, the sex was exceptionally hot.

Lainey rode out a leg-shaking climax, gyrating in my lap with my pulsing cock buried deep inside her, long enough for me to have my own mind-blowing orgasm at the same time. After she caught her breath, and while I was still recovering, she disengaged herself and hopped off.

She pulled up her panties and yanked down her short skirt. And then, standing in the aisle, she breathed out, "Wow, Nolan, that was amazing. I'm glad I took that study break."

I laughed. "Yeah, I bet."

We hadn't bothered to undress completely, having just yanked up or down what had been necessary. All I had to do was pull up my boxers and adjust my pants, which I did, but without bothering to zip up. I kind of wanted more, but we were awfully tight on time.

Ah, what the hell… I yanked Lainey down to my lap.

She pretended to protest. "Nolan—"

But I put a stop to that. "Shut up and let me kiss you, eh?"

That made her melt. "Oh, I love it when you talk Canadianisms."

"Silly girl."

I kissed her hard. Shit, I was still had a lot of pent-up energy. What was wrong with me? I'd just played a hard game *and* blown my load. Yet something was nagging at me. I felt like things were closing in, and I didn't like it or know why. I assumed that's why I wanted more sex.

I tore away from the kiss, long enough to ask, "Do you know how fucking gorgeous you are, Lainey?" She was fucking glowing, and I growled, "Fuck. I can never get enough of you."

She let out a sigh, and I nuzzled her neck until she relaxed into my arms like a gooey post-orgasm mess.

"God, I know, Nolan," she purred. "I feel the same way about you."

There was something in her tone, like a hint of underlying meaning in her remark.

What the fuck does that mean? Maybe we shouldn't have more sex.

I ignored my rising panic as she straddled me. And that's when, as I was sliding my nose along her collarbone and inhaling her, I realized something—it was my *own* feelings I was terrified of. But how could that be? I never let myself become too attached.

Dropping the idea of another round of sex, I asked, "When can I see you again?"

She tensed like I'd brought up something she'd been mulling over.

"Um, I'm not sure."

She hid her face in the crook of my neck. This wasn't Lainey, all meek and uncertain. But I sure as hell wasn't about to ask her what was bothering her. That might lead to me having to express myself, as in put my own heart out there on the line.

Fuck that. Been there, done that, and what did I learn? That it's easier to just fuck 'em and leave 'em.

"Tell me when," I pressed, keeping on the subject of sex, even though it wasn't happening now. But she didn't know that.

"I have to see you again." I reached down and cupped her warm and still-so-wet-for-me pussy, her panties a poor barrier. "Fuck, I need more of this...and soon. If the team wasn't due back any minute, I swear I'd bend you across this fucking aisle right now and have you one more time."

There actually was time, but that weird feeling of being trapped was holding strong.

Suddenly, not helping matters, Lainey said, "Hey, I have an idea."

I knew right away this wasn't about meeting up again for more sex. And she wasn't taking the bait for my bend-you-across-the-aisle suggestion—even if it had been a bluff—so this couldn't be good. I also had a suspicion her "idea" wasn't something new. It was something she'd been pondering for a while.

Gearing up for the worst, I moved my hand to the outside of her thigh, a safer area for what was becoming an unfortunately more serious talk.

Cautiously, I asked, "What kind of idea are we talking about here?"

She drew in a breath, then blurted out, "What do you think about coming to my graduation?"

"Uh..." *Shit.*

Lainey rushed on, like she could convince me by talking fast. "It's only a couple of weeks away, Nolan. And you'd only have to stay for that day. Unless, of course,"—her turquoise eyes met mine, and there was so much emotion, real emotion, in those depths—"you'd *want* to stay longer."

I went stone-cold still. "Babe, the playoffs are starting next week. I can't get away."

"Okay, so like I said, just stay for the day. I already checked the schedule, and there's not supposed to be a playoff game that Saturday."

"Lainey..." I loosened my grip on her, wishing she'd get off me. I was feeling way too constricted.

Winking down at me, trying to put on a brave front even though it was obvious I wasn't warming to her plan, she said coyly, "You know I won't be busy every second of that day. I'm sure we could get away."

Ah, the old lure-me-with-the-promise-of-sex trick, an oldie but goodie, and one that usually worked. I had to give her props for pulling out all the stops. Too bad it wasn't having an effect on me this time.

"I don't know," I hedged, hoping I could let her down easy before we reached a point of no return. "Your whole family will be there that day, eh?"

Not even my "Canadianisms" could make her smile then. We were definitely doomed.

"Yes, of course they'll be there, Nolan. That's the whole point. You've met my sister, but I want you to meet my parents."

Shit, too late. The point of no return had just been breached. And damn if she didn't look even more determined, her initial reticence evaporated.

I let go of her, my hands dropping to my sides. "What? Why would I want to do that?" I asked, alarmed.

Her face fell. Fuck, she was hurt, and it was my fault. Quickly, she schooled her expression to something more neutral. She knew I was getting antsy.

But how could I not feel boxed in? Attending a freaking life event with Lainey and her family sounded like commitment territory to me. And I avoid that shit at all costs. She knew that too. But she didn't know I had a damn good reason.

Still trying to play it cool, she smiled down at me so sweetly that it just about broke my heart. For where I knew this was headed…and how I knew I'd have to respond.

"Nolan," she said, trying hard to sound reasonable. "We can't keep it a secret forever that we've been hooking up. Sure, Aubrey may have issues with you, but my parents are different—"

"Your sister fucking hates me," I interjected as I tried to derail the locomotive heading for a brick wall.

"That's not true."

I gave her my best are-you-sure-you-want-to-go-there look, to which she replied, "It doesn't matter. Aubrey's bound to figure out there's something going on between us. Hell, I think Brent already suspects we've slept together. So graduation is the perfect opportunity to stop hiding and come clean."

"Uh, I don't know, Lainey."

I was at an impasse. I didn't want to end what I had with her, but I sure as hell wasn't ready to commit to a "real" relationship with her either. While I sat there, thinking of ways for us both to come out of this unscathed, sweet Lainey grew more and more excited, mistaking my silence for capitulation.

"My parents are going to love you," she squealed, scaring me further. "And you know your teammates will be all-in on the idea of us. With that many people in our corner, my stubborn sister will have no choice but to accept us as a couple."

Aubrey and her opinions were the least of my worries. "Hold up a minute, babe." I was trying to sound cool and casual, but I don't know. I guess, in looking back, I just sounded terse. "You need to relax," I said. "Go with the flow a little more."

"Relax? Go with the flow?"

I felt Lainey's anger begin to roll off her. And I knew she'd reached her boiling point when she jumped up off my lap. Not only is she impulsive and fiery in bed, but she's a spitfire outside of it.

"What exactly are you trying to say?" she ground out.

Oh, this next one was bound to get me into trouble. Still, I couldn't refrain from stating, "Look, we've hooked up what, *maybe* four or five times since New Year's Eve?"

"More like seven, Nolan. But who the fuck is counting, huh?"

"Does that include today?" I raised a brow. *Bad move.*

"Fuck you, Nolan." *Ooh, she's pissed now.*

I turned it down a notch, so I wouldn't end up with one of her heels in my head.

"Okay, then," I went on, all reasonable-sounding, or so I thought. "That's really not all that much time. And when you add in that most of those occasions were spent fucking—"

"That's because *fucking*, Nolan, is all you ever want to do," she yelled.

I slanted my head to the right and gave her a come-on-now look. "And you don't want the same?"

"Irrelevant." She waved her hand. "I want more now."

Bristling, I maintained, "We're not anywhere near where we would need to be to declare this thing between us as any kind of relationship."

Hands on her hips, she glared down at me. "Is that so? Even though we text and talk on the phone all the time. And don't even get me started on how many lonely nights on the road you call just to talk. Like, for hours, you bastard. Late into the night, even! And now you're telling me it all means nothing?"

She paused when I failed to reply. All those things *did* mean something, but I couldn't bring myself to admit it to her. I was too fucking spooked.

After a long beat of silence, she whispered, "Wait. I see what's going on. I'm nothing more than your Minneapolis hookup. That's all I am to you, a good time in the sack. I'm right, aren't I, Nolan?"

She wasn't, not at all, but I couldn't open my mouth to refute her claims. I just fucking could not.

When I didn't respond in any way, she started worrying her lip, biting down so hard I expected her to draw blood. There was none, and I was so fucked in the head that all I could think was, *damn, those wonderful, full, plump lips were wrapped around my cock fifteen minutes ago. I sure am going to miss them.*

"Nolan," she ground out. "Answer me, damn it!"

I gestured to the front of the bus, to where the driver would soon be back, as well as my teammates. "Look, the guys will be here any minute. You should probably get going."

"Are you blowing me off?"

I busied myself with straightening my dress shirt and tie, and finally zipping up my pants. I was being a real prick, I knew it, but I couldn't help myself. My fear of commitment had reached fever pitch. I knew this one could hook me. And I couldn't have that.

I've been down that road before, and boy did I ever get burned.

Never. Again.

"Nolan?"

I glanced up at her. She was still in the aisle, looking more forlorn than I'd ever seen her. She knew this was goodbye. Why prolong it?

"Take care of yourself, Lainey. We've had a good time, sure, but this can't go on forever. I truly wish you only the best."

She hissed in a breath as she fought back tears. "You know what, Nolan Solvenson?"

"What, Lainey?"

"You're a first-class, grade-A prick."

"So I am," I replied.

Swiping away tears that were now running down her cheek, she stomped off.

And now here I sit, all these months later, and finally having realized—crazily enough, in Marty Quick's studio—that letting her go was the biggest mistake of my life.

Just as I'm about to right that wrong, a text dings in from Brent.

Hey, man. What day you coming in for training camp? I'm thinking about having some of the guys over this Friday night for an end-of-summer gathering, just something small and mellow. Aubrey shouldn't mind. Since we got back to town her sister's been staying with us and those two have been so busy running around that Aubrey's barely been home.

Ah, so Lainey's in Nevada, not Pennsylvania. Good to know.

I edit the criteria on my laptop, changing flight schedules from *Toronto to Pittsburgh* to *Toronto to Las Vegas.* It's only Wednesday, so I can make it to Brent's party so long as I return within the next two days. Lainey's living at his house, meaning I can start wooing her right away. She'll have no choice but to talk to me, because really, where's she going to go?

When I find a flight for Thursday that fits my schedule, I text Brent back, *Hey, I'll be back in town tomorrow evening.*

Cool. See you Friday, he replies.

With everything set, I'm thinking things may actually work out. With a new spring in my step—shit, I love a challenge—I head to my bedroom to start packing. But as I'm throwing clothes into an open suitcase I tossed onto the bed, I glance over at the floor-to-ceiling windows and have to pause.

The view of the Toronto skyline, with the lake in the background, is usually stunning. Today, however, I can't see much of anything. The earlier heat and humidity ushered in a shit ton of rain, leaving the current state of affairs gray and dreary. It's oddly reflective of how I've been feeling lately.

I can't deny any longer that there's a void in my life since I ended things with Lainey. She's definitely someone special. I look at Brent and Aubrey and can't help but see how happy they are, especially since they overcame all the obstacles that once stood in their way.

"You can have that kind of happiness too," I murmur.

But can I, really?

There's a nagging voice in the back of my head that knows the real truth on why committing to Lainey—*truly* committing—isn't going to be such a snap.

Before we can ever move forward, she needs to know the reason why I am the way I am.

Shit, only a few select people know that. I keep my past a closely guarded fortress. One secret in particular virtually nobody knows about. That was the one I feared Marty Quick had uncovered.

Thank God he had no clue that I was once married.

WHAT IS THIS FREAKING SECRET?

LAINEY

On Friday morning, Aubrey and I embark on a spa date. We've had a bunch, and I am kind of tiring of them, but this one is much needed. For her because she needs a break from wedding planning, and for me because I've been stressing over not having a job. My obsessing over Nolan hasn't helped matters, but Aubrey doesn't need to know about that.

What's weighing on me is not simply what I heard during that damn Marty Quick interview. That would be crappy enough, but soon I'm going to have to deal with Nolan directly. Training camp is around the corner and he'll be moseying back into town any day now, if he hasn't arrived already.

Crap.

As my sister and I lie facedown on side-by-side massage tables, and while our muscles are deliciously kneaded and plied, I decide it's as good a time as any to uncover some info on Mr. No Commitment himself.

First, I'd like to know if he's back in town. And if he is, does Mr. I-Banged-Ten-Strippers-in-One-Night plan to attend Brent's little soiree this evening?

If so, I better get my kicking foot primed and ready.

"Mmm, so, Aubrey," I begin, fact-finding mission underway, "you seem very Zen about Brent's party tonight. You're really this okay with him being around that much alcohol?"

Last year, Aubrey was assigned by the Wolves to be Brent's "life coach." He was partying to the point of excess, as in he was fucking up his career. My dear sister swooped in and straightened him out. And in the process, they fell in love.

Cue the sappy music for my sister's fairy-tale romance.

And cue the sad *womp-womp-womp* for my lack of one.

Aubrey opens her turquoise eyes, so similar to mine that it sometimes freaks me out. You'd think we were twins or something. But we're not.

As she peers over at me, relaxed as could be, she says, "Brent's problems are long behind him, Lainey. I'm not worried at all. He knows when to stop."

"Well, that's good." I take a deep breath. Then faking an upbeat but hopefully nonchalant tone, I say, "So who all is coming to this party? Are all the guys back in town?"

Aubrey lets out a contented sigh as the masseuse works on what I suppose is a particularly achy muscle in her shoulder, probably from her and Brent trying out some new, crazy sex position. Brent has done a phenomenal job of bringing out the wild side of my sister. I heartily approve. She's much more laid-back than she used to be, kind of like how I'd be if I were getting some lately.

"I'm not sure who'll be there," Aubrey replies. "I know Benny's back in town. I talked to him yesterday, and he's definitely coming."

I'm not surprised she knows where Benny is and what he's up to. Those two are pretty tight buds. There was a time he was someone else to us, though, based solely on his resemblance to Chris Hemsworth.

I adopt a teasing tone and, remembering those days, state, "Oh, so he's just Benny to you now? No more Thor?"

Aubrey snickers. "He can still be Thor to you, Lainey."

"Good." I laugh. "And so he will remain. Just don't tell him his secret identity, all right?"

"My lips are sealed, sister dear."

We share a smile, and I know she'll never rat me out. Not that he'd care. Benny is as easy-going as they come. There was once a time even when Aubrey and Brent were considering setting me up with him. But though he's a fun-loving bear of a man, one who happens to look an awful lot like the hot Australian actor who plays Thor in the movies, my heart will forever belong to one man only—Nolan.

Speaking of which, since Benny plays left wing on Brent's line, meaning he's Nolan's linemate too, it gives me a perfect segue to casually inquire, "What about Nolan? Has he flown in from Toronto yet?"

"Yes, apparently he's made it back to our fine town. Brent mentioned it yesterday." Aubrey lifts her head and makes a drama of rolling her eyes and scowling at me. "I was trying to block it out, Lainey."

"God, what is up with you two? Why do you hate him so freaking much?"

Aubrey doesn't like Nolan all that much, though I have no idea why.

She sighs, and tries to assure me, "I don't hate him. Really, I don't."

"So what's the problem?"

"I just happen to think he's an overconfident, full-of-himself ass."

"Whoa, don't hold anything back there, Aubs. Tell me what you really think." I chuckle since she's not entirely wrong. "Still, even *you* have to admit he has many good qualities."

She snorts. "Like what?"

"First off, the man is sin personified. He has a lot to be confident about. Have you checked out that body of his lately?"

"Can't say that I have," she replies dryly. "And why would I? I only have eyes for Brent."

I resist the urge to gag, and instead set her straight. "For your information, Nolan is just as hard and sculpted as your precious Brent. *And* he has those awesome ice-blue eyes to boot." I let out a little shudder, the good kind. "That gaze of his just penetrates the hell out of me."

Aubrey stares over at me suspiciously. "That better be the only thing he's penetrating you with, Lainey."

"It is," I squeak out.

Hey, I'm not technically lying since I haven't been "penetrated" since April, not by Nolan or anyone else.

"But," I go on, tossing out a feeler to gauge the depth of Aubrey's dislike for my former fuck buddy, "if he and I ever were to hook up, would it be so awful?"

"Yes. It would. You may find him charming and gorgeous, and maybe you're right about that, but he's the last man I'd ever want to see you end up with."

Oh boy. This is going to be an uphill battle all the way…if we ever do work things out.

Better start climbing now. "For the sake of argument," I toss out, "why would it be so bad?"

"Nolan treats women poorly, so that's one big reason." *I can't argue with that.* "Plus, I get the impression he has a lot of secrets. I think that's why he's so shady about, well"—she huffs—"almost every damn thing. Did you know I once asked Brent why Nolan never gets serious with anyone he dates, and if something from his past is the reason for his bad behavior?"

I perk up. This could be the answer as to why Nolan is the way he is.

"What'd Brent say?" I cautiously inquire.

"He knew something, but he wouldn't tell me."

Deflated, I murmur, "That sucks."

"Yeah, apparently Brent made a promise to Nolan last summer to keep quiet about whatever the hell it was he shared with him. When I pressed Brent on it, he told me to go ask Nolan myself, if I was *that* curious."

Hope springs eternal, so I ask, "Did you? Ask Nolan, that is."

"Are you kidding me? No. I don't really care what his stupid secret is."

But I do, I want to yell out.

Instead of doing something that'll confirm my interest in Nolan, I change the subject.

"It's not important, anyway," I say, brushing it off. "I've just been really bored lately. That's why I'm even asking. I clearly have too much time on my hands, Aubs."

She nods, but looks confused.

I hurriedly go on, with what probably needs to be said, and done, anyway, "I think I need to start putting more effort into finding a job.

Nothing has come through with the placement department back at my school in Minnesota." I sigh. "You do know I officially expanded my search to nationwide, right? But I'd like to stay here. Which reminds me, do you know if the Wolves are hiring for any entry-level marketing positions? You really enjoy working for them, so maybe they'd be a good fit for me too."

After Aubrey's life-coaching gig ended, and after a few bumps in the road with her and Brent, she ended up being offered a consulting job with the Wolves.

She took it and loves it.

To my surprise, Aubrey confirms that she's already on it, as in she's been secretly helping me.

"Funny you should mention it, Lainey. I asked Brent just the other day if he could put in a good word for you. He didn't know of any pending openings in the marketing department, but he did mention the lady who runs it is named Mrs. Fielding. After he told me that, I looked her up in the employee directory."

"And...?"

"Turns out, I don't know her personally. But if you e-mail me one of your most recent résumés, I'll make sure she gets it. Even if it means printing the damn thing and marching it up to her office."

I love my sister. "I love you, Aubs," I say. "And thank you."

"I love you too, sweetie. And I think it'd be awesome if you worked for the team too. We'd have even more to talk about than we do now."

"Like there's not enough." I laugh, as my sister and I are *never* at a loss for words.

I sure hope Aubrey and Brent can help me land a job, but the fact remains I need something now, anything really.

With a resigned sigh, I say, "I'm going to look for something in the meantime. Like a part-time job to fill the void till something really good comes through."

"That makes sense," Aubrey replies.

Suddenly, an idea based on where I'm living strikes. "Hey, maybe one of those big resorts on the Strip could use another cocktail waitress. I hear tips are really good in casinos."

"Yeah, I've heard that too," Aubrey confirms. "And as to whether those places are hiring, I think they pretty much always need people."

"Let's hope so," I murmur.

Besides keeping me busy, and thus making sure my mind is occupied with thoughts other than Nolan, I also really need the cash. My savings account is near-depleted and my student loan payments are piling up. I'm thankful that Brent's been letting me use one of his many cars—plus I'm staying at his and Aubrey's place rent-free—but it's high time I start contributing to, at least, the food and gas parts of things.

After we leave the spa, I bid Aubrey adieu, then head on over to the Strip. My first stop is one of the largest Vegas properties. But, can you believe it, they're not hiring.

"Great," I murmur sarcastically as I leave, stepping back out into the heat.

I want to give up—it's hot and I don't really want to work at a casino—but I forge forward. I can be stubborn like that, and in this case it pays off. After three more stops at three more casinos, I get lucky and walk out of the last one with a skimpy cocktail waitress outfit and, more importantly, a shift for tonight.

Unfortunately, tonight is also Brent's party. And we all know I have plans for Nolan. Oh well, this new job may put a crimp in my plans to kick Nolan in the junk for his stripper-ing ways this summer, but it doesn't mean I'll miss the party entirely. Since I'm in training, my shift is supposed to end at midnight on the nose.

And I sure have taken notice of how the thigh-high boots that are part of my new uniform feature the pointiest of toes.

"So yeah," I murmur as I head for my car, smiling slyly. "You better cover those balls, buddy."

WHAT THE F*CK ARE YOU WEARING

NOLAN

Brent's party is in full swing, and the boys and I are gathered out on the back patio. I'm having a good-enough time. I mean, it's great to see the guys and all, many of whom I've not had contact with since winning the championship, but I've yet to run into Lainey.

And it's almost fucking midnight, goddammit!

"She's the reason I'm even here tonight," I mutter to myself, frustrated.

Brent, unfortunately, is within earshot, and promptly asks, "Who are you talking about, Solvenson? Sounds like you have a secret you're keeping from us. Like maybe you invited someone to the party, and you're waiting for her to show?"

Ha, if he only knew. I have a secret all right—that I spent the winter nailing his soon-to-be sister-in-law.

Benny is standing next to me and, upon hearing Brent's jab, gets right to ribbing me.

"Hey, Solvenson, you been holding out on us? You have, haven't you? I *knew* there was a reason why we didn't see much of you this summer." Glancing around, scanning the large sandstone patio and the surrounding gardens, like he's in on this with me, he says, "Who you looking for, anyway? Your secret girl's not here yet, is she?"

Brent appears to be particularly interested in my response, so it's no surprise when he piggybacks on Benny's interrogation.

"Yeah, Nolan, we're dying to know." Brent levels me with an assessing look. "Is someone supposed to meet you here? *Or* were you expecting to see someone you were pretty sure would *already* be here?"

The only two guaranteed attendees of the female persuasion are Aubrey—who's at this very moment sliding open a glass panel door in the back of the house so she can rejoin us—or her sister Lainey. Brent knows it wouldn't be Aubrey I'd want to see, which leaves only her sister.

Better fix this shit before I'm busted.

I rush to make up a cover story, winging it as I go along. "Yeah, there actually is someone I was hoping might stop by, someone I may have mentioned the party to."

"Oh, yeah," Benny jumps in. "Who'd you invite?"

Think fast, Solvenson. "Just some really hot flight attendant I met on the flight yesterday. I mentioned to her that she should stop by if she has nothing to do. That was after she made a point to tell me she'd be in town for a few day on a layover. She seemed like a wild one, but alas…." I muster my best faux disappointed sigh. "…I guess she had something better to do."

"Who had something better to do?" Aubrey, barging in on our bro powwow, wants to know.

"Nobody," I mutter.

She heard more than she's letting on, I know it. Sure enough, ten seconds later, she snarks, "Do you mean to tell me there's actually a woman out there who resisted the world-renowned Solvenson charm?"

Sarcastic little wench.

Hmm, I wonder if Lainey has been singing my praises. Positive words about me would definitely irk Aubrey.

"I guess even *I* can't win them all over," I snap right back at her.

"Win them all over?" Aubrey scoffs. "I thought your MO was simply to *fuck* them all over."

"Or just straight-up fuck them," Benny, the traitor, chimes in.

"Dude."

I give him a look, and he says, "Sorry, man."

Clearly, the bro code needs some fine-tuning; the summer break has left it lacking.

Aubrey, meanwhile, is suddenly busy murmuring something to Brent. I try to ignore her, but I do perk up when I overhear her say, "That was Lainey who was calling when I went inside before. She's running a few minutes late, but she should be here any minute."

"Cool," Brent says. "Did she say how her first night of training went?"

Training? She must've gotten a job. But what kind of marketing position requires training at night?

"Yeah," Aubrey replies, "she said it was a little tricky since she's never waitressed before. But I guess her tips were good, so she's sticking with it."

"That's great," Brent replies.

Hmm, so Lainey has a new job at a restaurant. That *is* great. I know her well enough that I'm sure she hasn't been happy sitting around Brent and Aubrey's place day in and day out, with nothing really to do. She's personable enough that I imagine she'll rake in some good money waitressing.

Benny asks where she's working, which I'm interested to find out too, but before Aubrey or Brent can reply, another player from our team comes over, interrupting our Lainey discussion.

"Hey, Nolan, how's it going?" Dylan Culderway, one of our best offensive-minded defensemen, shakes my hand, and then bestows quick *hellos* to everyone else.

Along with Brent and Benny, I count Dylan as one of my best friends. He's from Buffalo, which though in the States, isn't all that far from where I grew up in Ontario. Our proximity in birthplaces was the initial glue that bonded us together, but our friendship has evolved since.

"Things are good," I reply. "How's your summer been?"

"It's been great. Nice to have some time off after that Cup run, yeah?"

"You're not kidding."

He runs his hand over his closely cropped dark hair, making the sleeve of his black tee ride up and expose the start of a huge dragon tattoo that extends from his massive bicep, up over his shoulder, and across his back.

"Still, it's good to be back," he goes on. "I'm more than ready to hit the ice and start the new season. The break's been long enough."

"I hear ya," I concur. "I'm done with sitting around idle too."

Dylan and I are a lot alike, in more ways than just this one. We're serious dudes, quiet loners in some ways. Sure, we get along great with the guys, and we can party with the best of them, but no one can ever really understand us. Dylan's introspective, like me. And he doesn't share a lot, also like me. I sometimes wonder if he was done dirty by a woman—again, like me—or if he just naturally possesses a warrior's heart. In any case, he's not only a force to be reckoned with on the ice, he's a fighter outside the arena too.

One of the reasons we didn't see much of each other these past couple of months is that Dylan was traveling a lot, again like me. But whereas my trips were for fun, his were wrought with purpose. Something he doesn't talk much about, but everyone knows, is that his mother was a victim of domestic abuse. She unfortunately didn't get out in time and met an untimely end at the hands of her abuser. The guy was Dylan's stepfather. Awful, right? Poor kid was just a child at the time too. He witnessed a lot of the abuse, too much for a kid, and he was there that terrible, final night.

After his murderous stepfather was locked up for life, Dylan was sent to live with his grandmother. He decided to make his life about hockey, something he was already excelling at and happened to love. As time went on Dylan found another cause, one even closer to his heart—championing domestic violence victims. When he's not on the ice, he devotes a ton of time to that cause. It's how he spent his summer, traveling the globe, raising funds, and fighting for the rights of domestic violence victims.

He's a good dude, and we talk a little more now. Not about anything serious, just hockey shop talk. Aubrey, Brent, and Benny join in on the conversation too, but at some point it ends up just me, Benny, and Dylan standing around, shooting the breeze.

Brent and Aubrey were having trouble keeping their hands off each other and, thankfully, excused themselves to head indoors. After witnessing their shameless flirting, it doesn't take a rocket scientist to figure out why—they want to hook up.

I swear, those two are so fucking crazy in love that it's nuts.

A feeling of wistfulness washes over me, and I can't help but think of Lainey. I'm only half listening to the guys, mostly because I'm busy keeping an eye out for her. Aubrey said she was on her way home, so where the hell is she?

I check my phone. It's well after midnight.

I need to formulate a plan to extricate myself from the conversation so I can head to the front of the house and possibly catch her before she pulls into Brent's multicar garage.

That would afford us a few minutes alone to talk.

Turning to Dylan and Benny, I open my mouth to make an excuse for why I have to go, but before even one word is uttered, Benny lets out a low whistle, effectively shutting me up.

"Dude, check out Aubrey's sister," he says quietly. "I sure wouldn't mind tapping that just once."

Dylan nods in agreement, and I feel like punching them both. Of course, I don't.

When I turn around to see what's eliciting this kind of reaction from my teammates, I blurt out, "Jesus."

Lainey's decked out in a hot-as-fuck short black skirt and a flouncy white blouse. There's a black corset laced up over the top, creating a major push-up bra effect. Thigh-high boots, with pointy toes that look like they could seriously maim someone, complete the sexy ensemble.

"What the hell?"

I can't help it, and I don't care who sees, but my hungry gaze travels up her long legs, over her tiny waist, and across her luscious tits that are spilling out over the ruffled material of the frilly top.

Before anyone can stop me, and still not caring who sees what, I stride over to her.

"Oh, hey, Nolan," she says, all nonchalant-like, when I reach her.

She has to know an outfit like this drives me crazy. That's why she looks so smug. Oh well, she's right. Not only do I want to rip the sexy clothes off her, but the wicked things I'd do to her afterward would have her screaming out my name.

All that is forgotten, though, when I suddenly realize something,. And it starts bothering the crap out of me—Lainey doesn't seem the least bit surprised to see me.

"Did you plan this?" I gesture to her bar wench ensemble. "Because, really, what the fuck are you wearing?"

"Are you serious?" She glares at me, incredulous. "You think I wore this outfit because I knew *you'd* be here?"

"Yes."

She rolls her eyes. "You wish, Nolan."

"Who knows with you," I snap, defensive since I can't fucking think straight. "I wouldn't put it past you to wear something like this"—I wave my hand around in front of her, at the outfit muddling my mind—"purely to torture me."

Hands on her hips, she shakes her head. "Not that it's any of your business, you smug ass, but this happens to be my work uniform."

"What's your new job? Working the fucking corner?"

"Fuck you, Nolan."

I laugh. This is how we are. This back-and-forth snarking is like foreplay for us.

"Ooh, feisty." I rub my hands together, ready to go at it with her. "Hit me with some more, Lainey. I love it when you talk dirty."

"Ugh. I hate you, I swear!"

She growls at me then, but it's more cute than fierce. Lainey's a feisty kitten, not a tiger.

Even though we're well out of earshot of everyone, I check around to make sure no one is paying us any heed, or perhaps wondering why we're engaging in such a lively exchange, seeing as we're supposed to barely know one another.

Luckily, no one is paying any attention to us.

I relax, content in the knowledge that, really, the only two people who'd suspect something—or would care if there was something going on—are Aubrey and Brent. And they're still mercifully MIA, probably banging the shit out of each other this very second.

Good for them if they are. Lainey and I have time to hash this out.

Clearing my throat, I dial it back a notch, saying to her softly, "Look, I don't want to fight with you. It's just that you drive me nuts sometimes with the things you do."

She rolls her eyes. "How can you even say that so casually, Nolan? We haven't seen each other in months."

"And you have to admit that it totally sucks," I reply, laying it on the line.

Step one is admitting I missed her.

When she dips her head, hiding her pleased grin, I say, "Is that a smile I see, Miss Shelburne?"

"No," she retorts, but damn if she's not smiling ear-to-ear.

"You little liar, you're definitely smiling." I start laughing, seeing as I'm feeling pretty damn happy myself all of the sudden. "Don't deny it."

"Even if I am," she replies, "I still hate you."

"Ah, but the heat in your eyes tells a different story, my dear."

"Shut up. And quit giving me that look."

I feign innocence. "What look?"

"The look that says you think we're okay."

"We're not?"

"No!" She huffs, and gets right to reading me the riot act. "For your information, buster, you're not forgiven for dismissing me so rudely the last time we saw each other. You remember, Nolan," she growls.

Uh-oh, angry kitten is back.

"You surely haven't forgotten that night in Minneapolis, have you? What happened on the team bus?"

"Of course I haven't forgotten." I sigh. "And I feel really bad for how things went down. That's not how I planned to end things."

She raises a brow. "But you did plan to end things?"

I rake my fingers through my hair. "Fuck. I don't know anymore," I admit.

Step two is letting her know I don't have all the answers.

"I guess we should talk a little more about this," she says softly.

There's something akin to capitulation in her eyes, and I think, *good, she wants me back.*

But then again, this could also be a trap.

Shit, my trust issues are raising their ugly heads. Smacking those issues back down, before they compel me to say something stupid, I wave a hand at the sliding glass doors at the back of the house.

"If we want to talk, we should probably go inside."

She agrees immediately.

This is too easy. I wonder if she's up to something.

Dismissing my concern, we head into the house. I step inside first so I can check and make sure the coast is clear. We both know who we need to avoid.

"There's no sign of Aubrey or Brent," I whisper, holding my hand out for her to take it and step into the darkened kitchen with me.

"Come on," I continue when she steps in, albeit without my helping hand. "Let's go find a quiet place where we can talk."

"I know where we can go," she says.

I let her lead me then down a long hall on the first floor. I know from having been in this house so many times that she's taking me to a guest bedroom. It must be where she's staying while she's here.

Okay, so far, so good. Me alone in a bedroom with Lainey works for me. It's bound to lead to one thing and one thing only—hot sex.

And that my friends is step three in my plan—fuck her till she begs to pick up where we left off.

Lainey steps into the guest bedroom—her room—and beckons for me to join her.

Fuck, she looks hot. And now I have her alone.

I walk in, all set to make my move.

But, wait, what the fuck?

Lainey spins to face me, not looking happy at all.

What the fucking-hell-fuck? What happened to our truce?

I realize it's over and an all-out war when she casually tries to kick me in the fucking balls.

6

YOU DESERVE MORE THAN A KICK IN THE BALLS, NOLAN

LAINEY

"**A**re you fucking crazy?" Nolan is pissed as hell as he covers his junk. "What the hell do you think you're doing?"

I miss, and kick at him again.

He smoothly moves out of the way of the onslaught of my pointy-toed boot. It's kind of like he's avoiding a check, but one that could do irreparable harm.

"Strippers, Nolan?" I grind out, giving him the reason for this assault. "Really?"

"Oh, you heard Marty Quick's show," he states calmly, much too calmly.

That makes me more infuriated than ever. How dare he remain so cool and collected when I'm fuming!

I try to kick him again, but now that's he's onto me, he catches my ankle with ease.

"Quit trying to take out my junk, Lainey," he warns.

Ooh, he's as angry as I am. *Finally.*

"You deserve more than a kick in the balls, Nolan," I hiss. "Now let go of my ankle."

He smirks, but makes no move to let go, leaving me standing there tottering on one foot, while trying to grab onto the edge of a nearby dresser. I'd don't want to fall on my ass. That'd kind of blow any ass-kicking persona I have going here.

"Let go of me," I squeal as my arms pinwheel. So much for the ass-kicking 'tude.

"Are you sorry?" Nolan wants to know.

"Hmm, am *I* sorry?" I whip my head around to glare at him. "Quit being a dick."

He suppresses a laugh and, as I hop on one foot to stay balanced, I hiss, "This is not funny, Nolan."

He finally takes pity on me and loosens his hold enough that I can find purchase on the edge of the dresser.

"I'm waiting for that apology," he says softly once I'm steadied.

I peer back at him, having to twist at a weird angle since he still has hold of my ankle.

Well, I'm still defiant, pal.

"I'm only sorry I didn't make contact," I purr sweetly.

He raises a brow. "Do you really mean that? Possibly rendering me childless for the rest of my life was really your intent?"

"Oh, stop being so dramatic. I do feel a little bad. My only intent was to make a point—literally—not harm you for life."

Shaking my foot and unsteadying me again, he exclaims, "Look at these things! You could kill someone with a pointy toe like that.

Puncture a nad, for sure. Maybe even blow out a blood vessel—"

"God, stop! I get it, okay? I was wrong and I'm sorry."

Apparently, my giving in is not enough for Nolan. Instead of releasing me, he twists my foot this way and that, throwing me off-balance again.

"Nolan, don't," I beg, which is probably what he wants. "I'm going to fall." He probably wants that too.

But there's another concern now, at least for me. With my upper body splayed across the dresser, and him holding my ankle higher than before, my damn skirt is pushed up so high that he has to have a perfect view of my crotch.

Shit, I hope he can't see how wet my panties are becoming.

Okay, I'm hopeless, I know. But sparring with Nolan, not to mention how the position he's holding me in is reminiscent of ways he's held me in the past—mostly while we were gloriously naked—is turning me on.

But, alas, it's not the view that alerts him to my current ready-to-be-sexed-up state. No. It's the moan-y gasp I release when I pant out a desperate, "Nolan, *please.*"

He smirks. Oh, now he knows for sure. And if there is any doubt, it's erased when he glances at my panties. "Oh, Lainey, you are one bad girl."

"Shut up."

Looking smug, he releases me.

I maneuver to a seated position atop the dresser and murmur, "I hope you enjoyed the show."

"I did, Lainey, I enjoyed it very much."

When he then wedges his hard body between my legs, there goes my last scrap of willpower to resist him. I let out a wanton groan because, as established, I'm hopeless. I rest my back against the wall, and since I have no shame and I freaking want him like crazy, I line up my center with his junk. Yep, the same junk I was trying to kick minutes ago.

What the hell was I thinking, anyway? Wanting to harm him like that...

But wait, what the hell am I thinking now?

"What are we doing, Nolan?" I ask softly.

With one brow raised and pressing into me, he says, "Isn't it clear?"

"Um, I don't think—"

"Don't think, Lainey, just go with it."

He hoists my leg up over his shoulder and circles his hips. "Oh, Nolan..."

"Lainey, Lainey—"

"Whoa, wait!" I remember where we are and push him away. "Aubrey and Brent are around here somewhere."

He kicks the door closed. "I don't think we need to worry about them."

Our eyes meet then and, though there are so many unspoken words, the message is clear. His searing blues burn with desire. Does he see the same in mine? He must, because nothing stops him now.

He reaches down and glides a finger along my soaked panties, leaving me crying out in pleasure. As he brushes over my swollen clit, again and again, each pass harder than the one before, I start to make a lot of noise.

"Shh, Lainey," he whispers in my ear. "You have to keep quiet, or someone *will* figure out we're in here."

"I don't know if I *can* keep quiet." I groan as he pushes my panties aside and gently massages my clit between his thumb and index finger.

"And that's not helping," I add.

"Should I stop?"

"Don't you dare."

Despite my encouragement to keep going, out of the blue he stops what he's doing, leaving me aching for more of his skilled touch.

"That wasn't an answer," he says, his mouth set.

"Stubborn man," I murmur.

He'll win. He always wins. He's done this before—teasing me, taunting me, making me beg for more. But tonight we don't have time for all that. All I want is to feel him inside me—it's been *so* long—so I may as well give in.

"Nolan, stop teasing me." I rotate my hips so that his fingers, wedged in my undies, provide some much-needed friction.

When he feels how much wetter I am, he lets out a growl.

I've got him now.

The power shifts, and he's suddenly the hungry, vulnerable one. But wait, maybe not, since the next thing I know, my panties are torn right down the middle.

He drops to his knees, and says, "I'm going to make you come so hard."

His hot breaths tickle my bare lips, and I gush out, "God, yes!"

I push toward him, and he's on me, devouring my pussy like it's his last meal. When I reach the brink, he rises to his knees and takes out his rigid cock.

"Look how fucking hard you make me," he says, urging me to take him all in.

I look. In fact, I stare. And maybe I drool a little. Finally, I say what I want— "Give it to me, Nolan."

But then he stills, and says, "Are you sure, Lainey?"

He's giving me a chance to back out, because we've settled nothing. Hell, ten minutes ago I was ready to kick him in the junk. But I have no control around this man. I never have. And apparently I never will, seeing as the next words out of my mouth are, "Yes, I'm sure."

"You still on birth control?" he quickly gets in.

"Yes."

He grabs my ass and impales me with one commanding thrust.

"Nolan, fuck, yes." *God, I've missed him.*

He starts grinding into me, pushing me back, so I use the wall behind me for support. I give him back just as much, though. But when he tosses my legs up over his shoulders and pistons into me like a machine, I relinquish all control.

"Fuck me as hard as you can," I say. "Give me all you got."

He does, and our bodies say everything our mouths cannot. Yanking down the front of my top with his teeth, my breasts spill over and he's on them like a hungry beast, sucking and nipping.

The dresser bangs against the wall in rhythm with his angry thrusts, and when I start to moan loudly, he shoves two fingers in my mouth to shut me up.

"Taste yourself," he rasps in my ear.

Yes.

I suck and lick and get fucked till I explode around him. Nolan's wet fingers leave my mouth so he can play with my clit and I come again, joining him in his release.

"Shit, that was hot," he pants against my shoulder a minute after we're finished.

I can only nod. Coming down from my own sexual high, I'm pretty much useless. After Nolan pulls out, he takes it upon himself to clean us both up with a towel he finds on my messy floor.

"You're so good to me," I murmur when he slides my ruined panties down and off my legs.

But then I remember what I was originally angry about.

"Wait a second." I smack at his hand and he drops the towel.

"Ow, what the fuck is wrong now?"

I glare at him, and he takes a step back and quickly zips up his jeans. Surely to protect his dick from any further assaults I may have planned. He needn't worry. All I want to do is talk.

After adjusting my shirt back into place to cover my boobs, I straighten my skirt and slam my legs shut. There will be no more sexing till I get some answers.

"Is it true, Nolan?"

He eyes me warily. "Is what true?"

"You know what." I shoot him a look that says he better know.

I'm referring to the stripper story, but he seems really panicked, more so than he would be for whoring around when we weren't even together. I know then that the bigger secret Aubrey mentioned must be huge. And damn it, I'm going to find out what it is, even if it freaking kills me. For now, though, I focus on the first thing we need to address.

"Marty Quick said you banged ten strippers in one night."

"Oh, that."

"Don't look so freaking relieved, Nolan."

"I'm not," he insists.

I fold my arms across my chest. "Well, I'm waiting for an answer."

With a sigh, he comes clean. "It wasn't ten. It was nine. And it occurred over the course of two days, not one night." He squares his shoulders and puffs out his chest. "I'm amazing, babe, yes, but I am still human."

That cocky motherfucker!

I try to kick him again, though not in the junk this time. I've decided I like that part of him far too much. It'd be a tragedy to put it out of commission. Still, he's way faster than me and stops me long before I make contact with my new target—his thigh.

"Quit trying to kick me, Lainey," he says, irritated.

I point at him. "We just had unprotected sex, mister. You better not have given me some gnarly disease."

"I'm clean," he assures me. "I always use condoms with everyone but you. Plus, I was tested just last month."

I breathe out a sigh of relief.

"What about you?" He raises a brow. "*You* better not have given *me* anything."

I've not been with anyone but him since the first time we were together. But I can't tell him *that* and give him a bigger head than he already has.

I instead go with, "You're fine, Nolan. I've only had protected sex too."

He swallows hard. And wait a minute. Is that hurt I see in his ice-blue gaze?

I watch him closely, and then ask, "Nolan, you don't care if I screw around with other guys, do you?"

"Lainey, I…" He runs a hand through his dark hair, looking uneasy.

"Well?" I press.

"Of course I care."

He cares? Wow, what does this mean? I blow out a breath and cautiously inquire, "So what happens now?"

"I guess this is probably as good a time as any to bring up some things I've been thinking we really need to talk about." He takes a deep breath. "Maybe if I share with you certain things about me, it'll make more sense as to why I am the way I am."

Wow, this is as real as we've ever gotten, and it's totally out of left field. How we've gone from me trying to inflict bodily harm on him, to us having amazing sex, and now to him ready to bare his soul is beyond me. But I'm rolling with it.

"Okay," I say softly. "I'm listening."

After a long beat of silence, his eyes find mine. "First of all, you should know *you're* the reason I came back to Vegas early."

Wait, what? "It is?"

"Yes."

This is a good sign. Maybe our little hookup isn't just a tale of two people insanely attracted to each other and nothing else.

He tenses, and I think that's it. He opens his mouth, but shuts it just as fast.

"Nolan," I say on a frustrated sigh.

I think I'm losing him, but then he gives me the kind of look that says he's about to tell me everything.

Sure enough, he begins with, "Lainey, back when I was a teenager I made a huge, stupid mistake—"

Rap, rap, rap!

Three staccato knocks on the door silence him instantly.

"Fuck!"

Just when I was about to get some answers from this man.

"Lainey, are you in there?" a woman's voice asks from the other side of the door.

Double fuck!

"It's Aubrey," I mouth to Nolan with a roll of my eyes.

"Here, quick." I jump down from the dresser and start hustling him toward the big walk-in closet on the other side of the room. "Get in there," I say. "And don't come out till she's gone."

He tries to protest, but only for a second. He knows there's no other option.

Once Nolan is safely hidden inside the closet, I straighten my clothes.

And then I open the door.

7

I DID *NOT* NEED TO HEAR THAT!

NOLAN

uck. Looks like I'm stuck in this stupid closet for however long it takes for Lainey to get rid of Aubrey. At least it's roomy in here.

As I lie back on the carpeted closet floor. I lace my fingers behind my head and hunker down for the long haul. I have sisters, so I'm well aware that girls can talk for-fucking-ever.

First thing I hear Aubrey blabbering on about is shit about the party, shit I'd rather not hear. "There are a lot of cute players out there, Lainey. What are you doing in here? You should come back outside for a while."

I resist the urge to growl and give myself away, but one thing for sure—Lainey better not go out to that party in *those* clothes. Her outfit was hot-as-fuck as it was, but minus the panties it's positively scorching. I don't need my teammates checking out her shaved pussy if she happens to bend the wrong way.

But, wait. I have no claim on Lainey. We were too busy sexing each other up to set any parameters on where we go from here. And just when I was about to share with her why I'm so damn commitment-phobic, irritating Aubrey shows up.

Maybe it's for the best, a little voice inside my head whispers.

I'm quick to jump on any out and this is a perfect one, so I agree with the voice. Lainey and I are back to having sex, and since I see no reason why it won't continue, I figure we can just carry on same as before. Back to the way it was—no commitments, no declarations of how much we mean to one another, and certainly no sharing dark secrets from the past.

I care for Lainey, yes, and probably more than I should, but now that I'm faced head-on with committing myself to her, I'm right back where I was before.

"Why are *you* not out at the party?" I hear Lainey ask Aubrey. "Isn't Brent going to miss you if you two are apart for, like, more than five minutes?"

I suppress a chuckle. I love that Lainey has no problem giving her sister a hard time about Brent. It's one of my own favorite pastimes, and it's good to know someone has been picking up the slack.

"Ha ha," Aubrey retorts dryly. And then in a lower voice, but one I unfortunately hear loud and clear, Aubrey says, "We're actually fine with a little time apart, seeing as we were just *together.*"

I roll my eyes. Is this how girls talk, in code? Why not just say they went off and fucked?

Lainey's just as bad, dragging out the suspense. "What? Are you saying you were just together-together?"

Together-together? More like fucking-fucking.

"Uh-huh," Aubrey replies, giggling.

Lainey then asks in a hushed tone, "How did you manage to get away when Brent's the host of the party?"

Hell, I don't need to hear anymore of this shit. But hear more, I do, lucky me. I get to be privy to *all* the details of how Aubrey and Brent snuck off to the laundry room, where Brent proceeded to fuck her hard against the washing machine.

"Too bad it wasn't on," Lainey says.

"Right," Aubrey replies. "But the sneaking off still made it fun. No one suspected a thing."

I raise my arm and mouth, "I did."

"Still, I have to say it was a little quicker than I would've liked," Aubrey continues in a breezy voice. "Still totally hot, though."

More giggles ensue, and I think, *shit, Brent must have some kind of skill to turn the ice princess into a silly schoolgirl like this.*

"How quick was quick?" Lainey asks once all the giggling has subsided.

Do women really discuss sex in this kind of detail? All I know is I'd never ask Brent, "Oh, hey, man, did you time how long you fucked Aubrey last night? Twelve minutes and twenty-four seconds of actual penetration, eh? Let me pull out my own performance charts so we can compare."

Yeah, that would never happen.

But women are obviously different, as Aubrey proves when she replies, "Way quicker than usual. Brent finished pretty fast. It was more the thrill than anything else, you know? That's really why we snuck off. To see if we could get away with it."

"I hear ya," Lainey says.

Aubrey sighs. "Only thing is I'm kinda sore now from not being completely ready. Brent was a little rougher than usual too. I guess because it was so fast and hot. Not that I'm complain—"

Fuck, I can't listen to another word. I actually cover my ears, like a damn kid. But seriously, I do not need to hear anything more about Aubrey's sore pussy. Though it does make me wonder just how big Brent is. Surely not bigger than me, right? I mean, I've seen him naked in the locker room, but it's not like he's been hard any of those times. Plus, straight men generally don't make a habit of checking out each other's junk. At least this straight man doesn't. Though I might be now.

"I'm sure Brent will make it up to you later tonight," Lainey is saying to her sister, all consoling-like, when I uncover my ears.

I can't help but feel a little smug that though Lainey and I were rather quick ourselves, I made sure she was completely ready before I got my dick wet. Then again, Lainey is pretty much *always* ready when we're around each other. Hell, that's one reason we can never restrain ourselves.

"Yeah," Aubrey says dreamily, "I'm sure he will."

I try not to throw up. But I sure as shit perk up when Aubrey next says, "Hey, what about you?"

"Um, what do you mean what about me?"

"Well, I've been meaning to ask you since you got here, what ever happened to that guy at school? The one you were seeing last spring?"

"Um..."

"You have to know who I mean, Lainey. The secret man you were obviously having amazing sex with, all while keeping him hidden from everyone."

Shit, that would be me.

I'm extremely curious to hear Lainey's response. She won't tell Aubrey I was her secret guy, but she may reveal something that'll give me a better idea of where her head's at right now, especially after what just happened between us.

"Oh," Lainey replies slowly, already sounding evasive. "That never amounted to anything much. Actually, it turned out to be nothing more than a random fling."

Random fling? What the fuck?

Look, I may not be ready to fully commit, but I'm a selfish bastard. For her to speak so dismissively of what we had together kind of fucking hurts. Then again, maybe she's just making light because she knows I can hear every word.

"Sometimes a fling can be just what the doctor ordered," Aubrey says understandingly. "And that's why we should get you back out to the party, like right away. Who knows, maybe you'll find a new random fling."

No fucking way! I almost roar. But then I remember I'm not supposed to be hearing any of this.

Thankfully, Lainey replies, "I'm not looking to hook up, Aubs."

I breathe out a sigh of relief.

"Okay, but let's still get back out there before everyone leaves."

Lainey, all cagey-like, says, "Um, yeah, sure, but can you give me a minute to throw on a pair of boy shorts under this skirt. I was about to put on pajamas when you came in, and I already took off my underwear."

I smirk. *Nice save, Lainey, even if it does sound a little lame.*

I'm glad she's covering up. I'd lose it if Lainey were planning to head back out there commando.

Still, is she really leaving me here in her closet?

Aubrey says to her sister that she'll wait for her out in the hall. Meanwhile, I stand, all set to slip back into the room and catch Lainey before she goes.

When I push open the closet door, however, she's already gone.

"Shit."

I'm not up for more partying, and I'm certainly not going to chase Lainey all over the house.

I give up, murmuring, "Fuck. I may as well just go home."

NOLAN ON THE ICE MAKES ME REALIZE SOMETHING

LAINEY

Over the next couple of weeks, I don't see much of Nolan, which may seem strange since he lives only a few doors down from me. It's not a matter of missed connections, however. No, we're *purposely* avoiding each other, even after the hot sex in my bedroom. Actually it's *because* of the hot sex in my bedroom that we're staying out of each other's way.

See, if we hook up again, we'll have to talk.

And if we don't hook up again, but are in each other's presence, we'll still have to talk.

What the hell am I saying? We'll especially have to talk then. With no sex to distract us, we'd have to discuss our relationship...or lack thereof.

Shit, I don't even know what I really want, not anymore. It's why avoiding each other has been the best course of action. I guess in some ways I'm as fucked up as Nolan. That's why I left him in my bedroom the night of Brent's party. Once he was relegated to the closet, and I was away from him, I finally could think straight. And as Aubrey was gushing over her and Brent's sneaky laundry room encounter, I realized I was mad at myself for having sex with Nolan. I mean, how could I go from being so mad at someone, the very person I had every intention of kicking in the balls, to having that same person balls deep inside of me?

"Good question," I murmur as I flip through one of Brent's hockey magazines. "You're as mixed up as he is."

Needing to focus on something else—the hockey mag just isn't helping—I glance around the living room. I'd like to talk with someone, but no one is home. Aubrey is working over at her office in the Desert Sports Complex, and Brent had an early morning practice in the same place.

The empty house makes me wish I wasn't off from work today. That's why I've been lazing around and perusing magazines I have no interest in. Well, maybe I have a little interest. Seems having so many hockey people in my life is making me love the damn sport.

I resume flipping through the magazine, skimming over an article on which teams to watch this upcoming season. The Wolves are at the top of the list, no surprise there. I move on to a report on training camp, which is back in session around the league. And then I get to a bunch of short bios on all the current players, including Nolan.

My heart rate picks up when I peer at his picture. God, I have such intense feelings for that man. Still, I don't know if I want from him what I did last spring, namely a commitment.

I'm just not sure he *can* commit.

Though there is something I've been insanely curious about since the party—what it was he about to tell me when Aubrey inadvertently interrupted him.

What the hell happened when he was a teenager?

What sort of huge mistake did he make?

And how's that affecting us now?

It must be, in some way, since he said me knowing would help explain his behavior.

"I bet it was a relationship that ended badly," I mutter out loud.

Since there's no way of knowing till Nolan feels like opening up again, and who knows when that will be, I toss the magazine onto the sofa and bite out a curse.

But then I hear, "Ooh, sounds like someone's pissed over something," and I just about jump out of my hide.

Someone's in the house with me!

Jumping up, I pick up the magazine and whip it at the intruder.

Like that's going to hurt him. Maybe if he's a fly.

It's not a fly, it's just my future brother-in-law in the entryway. And my magazine missile missed him by a mile.

Crumpling back down to the sofa, I breathe out, "Shit, Brent. I'm sorry I threw something at you, but you scared the crap out of me."

"Clearly." Chuckling, he picks up the magazine. Holding it aloft, he says, "Next time you might want to throw something a little more formidable. The worst damage this thing could do is *maybe* give someone a nasty paper cut."

I start to laugh. "It was all I had." And then I ask, "What are you doing home so early, anyway?"

Stepping over to the sofa and placing my magazine-weapon on the coffee table, he informs me, "Practice ended a little sooner than usual."

"Oh, okay."

He plops down on a plushy chair across from me and takes in my ripped jeans and off-the-shoulder ivory sweater. "No work today, I take it?"

I've been picking up a lot of extra shifts lately and often when Brent's coming in from practice, I'm on my way out, clad in my waitress attire and ready to work another ten-to-twelve-hour day.

"Can you believe I'm actually off?" I say. "Shocking, I know."

"It is, Miss Workaholic," he replies, chuckling as he glances down at his phone, where a text is dinging in.

"It's Aubrey," he murmurs distractedly as he reads the text. After a few secs, he looks up and informs me, "Looks like she has to work later than usual today. We recently called up a couple of new guys from our minors system, and management must want her to meet with them to make sure their heads are where they're supposed to be before the regular season starts."

Aubrey used to provide—to Brent only—consulting, counseling, motivation, and whatever else was needed to keep him on track. That was her role as Brent's life coach. But then they fell in love and her position ended, until the team rehired her in her current position. She's now responsible for making sure *all* the guys stay focused on playing good hockey.

Luckily for her, and especially since Brent would never stand for it, she no longer has to live with her clients. She works from her office in the Desert Sports Complex, where the Wolves practice and play home games.

"Thanks for letting me know about Aubrey," I say. "I probably would've wondered where she was come dinnertime." I pick up my Kindle, which is never far out of reach. "Looks like I'll be getting in a lot of reading time today, which is excellent since my book boyfriends have been highly neglected lately."

Brent laughs. "Sounds like a plan Aubrey would approve of."

"Definitely."

Between Aubrey and me always gushing over our latest reads, he's grown accustomed to our reading addictions, book boyfriends included.

I'm all set to start my reading marathon, but it seems my book boyfriends may have to wait. Brent is making no move to leave. In fact, he's staring over at me like he wants to ask me something.

Crap, I hope it's not about Nolan. He's been suspicious about us ever since he caught me sneaking into the house New Year's morning, after spending the night at Nolan's having sex everywhere. I think Brent was onto me.

I breathe a sigh of relief when he simply asks, "You plan on reading all day and into the evening?"

"It wouldn't be the first time," I inform him.

"Huh, okay, but what if I told you there might be something more fun for you to do this evening?"

"More fun than reading? Hush your mouth!"

"Maybe not more fun than reading," he concedes, laughing, "but pretty close."

I set my Kindle aside...for the moment.

"This I gotta hear. What's this great, fun thing going on tonight? Is there another party in the works?"

"No, no more parties. But there does happen to be an exhibition game at seven. I could have a ticket waiting for you. That is, if your book boyfriends won't mind you leaving them for a while."

"I think they'll understand," I reply.

Even though preseason games count for nothing when it comes to the standings, I jump at the chance. Watching Nolan do his thing on the ice is one of my favorite things to do. And it's been a while since I've seen him play. We may not be together, and I'll never be mistaken for any kind of hockey expert, but I still can appreciate how skilled Nolan is.

That dark, brooding man just looks really good on the ice, okay?

"So is that a yes?" Brent asks.

"Yep," I confirm. "I'd love to go."

"Great." He stands. "Let me go make the call."

The seat Brent procures for me is amazing. I'm in the first row on the side where the Wolves shoot twice. Since the team is the reigning Stanley Cup champ, there are a lot of people in attendance, preseason be damned. Everyone is pumped, including me. I stand and cheer, like a crazed lunatic, every time the Wolves point up a point. And when Nolan scores a gorgeous goal late in the third that puts the Wolves up by one, I can't refrain from sharing my excitement with the person seated next to me.

"Oh my God, I think we're definitely going to win this one," I gush excitedly to a girl who's been to my left the entire game. She appears to be here alone, like me. I thought about talking with her earlier, but I was too immersed in the game—and Nolan—to strike up a conversation.

"Yeah, I think we will." She smiles over at me like she's happy I finally said something.

"I'm Lainey, by the way."

I hold out my hand, and she shakes it daintily.

"I'm Eliza," she says.

"I totally should've introduced myself earlier, seeing as we've been sharing space all night." I gesture to our seats and she nods, looking down and smiling.

"Aw, that's okay," she says. "The game's been pretty engrossing."

"It has."

Eliza is shorter than me and a bit curvier. There's a definite cuteness about her. Maybe it's the way she's wearing her strawberry blonde hair pinned up, all messy-like, or perhaps it's the sparkle in her emerald eyes. Whatever the case, I warm to her immediately. It also feels good to have someone other than Aubrey and Brent to talk to.

"Are you here all alone?" I ask.

I then realize how creepy that sounds, and amend, "Oh, crap. I don't mean that in any weird way. Like, I'm not trying to pick you up or anything."

That makes her crack up. "Well, you are very pretty, so if I swung that way I'd definitely let you."

Now we're both laughing, and I think I may have just made a friend.

"So," I continue, "let me word that a little differently. You're clearly here alone, so I guess what I'm asking is if you're here for someone on the team…or if you're just a totally rabid Wolves fan?"

"I'm not here for anyone," she replies. "And I don't know about the rabid part, but I am a fan. Though, I kind of have to be."

Ooh, now I'm really curious what her story is.

"Why's that?" I inquire.

"Coach Townsend is my dad."

"Oh wow, no way." I glance over at the Wolves' bench, to where her dad is currently barking out what is no doubt a defensive strategy to maintain the lead during the final few minutes of play.

"Coach T seems like a really nice guy," I go on, since from all accounts he is. "He's a really great coach, that's for sure."

"So they say," Eliza replies. There's an unmistakable look of pride on her face as she glances over at her dad. Then she turns back to me, and says, "This is kind of new for me, watching a Wolves game. Last season I missed pretty much every one, except for the ones that were broadcast nationally."

"Were you living somewhere else?"

"I was," she confirms.

I sense she's about to elaborate, but instead, she murmurs, "I was away at college."

"Oh yeah, where at?"

"Georgetown. You know, in DC."

Hmm, her responses are so clipped-sounding, like this is a sore subject. I sense Eliza Townsend may have some secrets. But it's none of my business. I won't pry, seeing as I've just met her.

In a tone I hope sounds casual, I remark, "Wow, that's a really good school."

"Yeah, it is. I liked it a lot too."

Now she sounds sad. Definitely, there's a secret.

"Did you graduate, then?" I ask. "Is that why you're back?"

"No." She laughs nervously. "I actually *should* be graduating this year, but I took a semester off this past spring." She starts talking really fast then, and I sense it's to divert me away from the real reason she left school. "I kept changing majors too. My dad was ready to strangle me. But it doesn't matter now. I'm back here, finishing up at UNLV." She quickly, and oddly, adds, "I just really missed the warm weather."

The weather seems like an odd reason to uproot your whole life so close to graduation, but, again, it's none of my business. As if to underscore that point, she looks away, making it clear this discussion is over.

With my seat neighbor preoccupied with her own thoughts, I take the opportunity to steal a glance over at Nolan. He's coming off the bench and onto the ice, and all I can think is, *damn, he looks good.* Even if the man does drive me nuts half the time—or more like, most of the time—I can't deny there's something about him that makes me think it may be worthwhile pursuing something with him.

"Are you in school?" Eliza asks out of the blue, breaking me away from my confusing thoughts on Nolan.

Tearing my gaze from the sweaty and hot-as-hell forward who's clearly worming his way back into my heart, I reply, "No. I graduated this past spring."

"Where'd you go?"

"I was at the University of Minnesota."

Her eyes widen. "Oh wow, that's a long way away. Did you find a job out here in Vegas?"

"Right, I wish." I shake my head, indicating a big, fat *no.* "I did get a job recently, but sadly it's nothing career-related."

"What are you doing?"

"Waitressing at one of the casinos."

"Ah."

I take a breath, and start verbal vomiting, sharing probably too much. "Yeah, I'm staying out here with my sister and her fiancé. At least, for a while. They've been really wonderful, but I don't want to take advantage, you know? It's just that this job market sucks. Once I find a real job, though, I plan on paying them back for everything. I *was* living back east with my parents earlier this summer, but they were driving me crazy."

Eliza, not one bit phased by my rambling—yeah, we're definitely going to be friends—looks over at her dad on the bench and says,

"Yeah, parents have a way of doing that sometimes."

I know from hearing Nolan and Brent talk that Coach Townsend can be a real stickler for discipline. I bet Eliza changing majors and switching schools is giving him an ulcer, hence her heavy sigh. But soon she's back to all smiles and focusing on a new line of conversation.

"So," she says, "your sister and her fiancé... Are they big hockey fans too?"

Ha, wait till she hears this one.

"Um, you could say that. My sister's fiancé is the one who got me the ticket for tonight's game."

"Well, it's a really good seat," Eliza says, pondering. "So I'm guessing he's either a player or someone pretty high up in management."

"He's not in management," I reply.

Before Eliza can question what my vague non-answer could mean, our attention is drawn to the ice. Play has resumed, and it's really freaking exciting!

"Wow, the game's really opening up," Eliza remarks as the puck is worked from one end of the ice to the other, back and forth, over and over.

"It sure has," I agree.

Regulation is almost over, and though we've maintained the lead, it's still only by one goal. It's no surprise then when the opposing team pulls their goaltender and adds an extra attacker.

"So who's your sister's fiancé?" Eliza finally gets around to asking. She nods to the players currently on the ice and says, "Is he out there right now?"

I point to where Brent is winding up, about to take a shot at the other team's empty net.

"She's engaged to that guy right there," I state proudly.

Goal!—the big scoreboard above center ice flashes in giant black and red neon lettering, the Wolves' colors, spelling out G-O-A-L! There are bells and whistles sounding all around us, and an announcer is yelling enthusiastically over the intercom that, "Brent Olll-i-veeeeer just shoots and scores!"

"Oh wow, your sister's engaged to Brent Oliver, huh?" Eliza turns to me then, green eyes widening as recognition dawns. "Wait a second, I know who you are. I've seen you in pictures with Brent and Aubrey. You're her sister, right?" I nod, and she muses, "Wow, now that I know I can really see the resemblance. It's uncanny, actually."

"Yeah, we hear that a lot."

Most people know Aubrey from the many pictures circulating around of her with Brent. Because we look so similar, people do sometimes confuse us. It really freaks them out when the three of us are photographed together.

The game ends with a Wolves victory, and people begin filing out of the arena.

Eliza stands. "I guess I better get going," she says, kind of sadly. "It was really fun talking with you, Lainey. Who knows? Maybe I'll see you around."

She turns to go, but I sense she wants to keep in touch. Maybe she just isn't sure how to go about it. But I say, *let's get this friendship started.* I'm even up for hanging out with her more tonight. God knows I have nowhere to go. We could grab a coffee back in the lounge by the locker room and work on becoming friends.

Stopping her before she takes off, I call out, "Eliza."

She turns back to me. "Yeah?"

"I was thinking if you don't have any plans right now, you're more than welcome to come with me back to the family lounge. I drove in with Brent so he's my ride home and I have to wait for him. Otherwise, I'd say let's go anywhere. But we'll have plenty of time to hang. I'm sure Brent will be tied up for a while. The media will want to interview him in the locker room about that goal at the end of the game."

"Yeah," Eliza agrees, "I'm sure they will."

"So what do you think? You up for drinking all the free coffee in the lounge? We'll be right by the locker room, meaning if we position ourselves just right by the door we'll have a really good chance of seeing a half-naked player walk by."

I can tell before she even opens her mouth that it's a no-go. But I wonder why since she looks like she'd really *like* to join me in ogling hot hockey players.

Sadly, my guess is right and she says, "I'd love to hang with you, Lainey. Really, I would. I mean, shit, I'm always up for admiring hot hockey player butts."

"We could rate them even," I throw out as incentive. "Just not Brent's. That would be weird."

Chuckling, she says, "Another time, I promise. But we'll have to hide me from my dad."

"Huh? Why?"

"He'd totally flip if he saw me back there."

Confused, I say, "Really?"

She sighs. "It's a long story, but the bottom line is he doesn't trust any of his players around me. Not all of them, of course, but he's wary of a few." *I wonder if Nolan is on that list.* "It's ridiculous, I know. I swear no matter how old I get—and I'm freaking twenty-one—nothing's ever going to convince that man that his little girl doesn't need protecting."

"Aw, you have to admit, that is kind of sweet."

"More like annoying." She rolls her eyes. "But anyway, if you know someone other than Brent on the team, I'm sure whoever it is would love to hang with you while you wait for your ride."

Ha, do I know any players other than Brent? I certainly do. I know a certain dark-haired, piercing blue-eyed right winger extremely well, like in a biblical sense.

"Yeah"—I nod, not ready to share *that* much information—"I'm sure I'll find someone to hang with."

"Well, like I said, it was really great meeting you."

"You too, Eliza."

She takes out her phone. "Do you want to maybe exchange numbers before I go? We can do something some other time. The player butt-ogling, or anything really, would be fun."

I laugh. "Sure. Sounds like a plan." I take out my phone and give her my number, and she sends me a text so I'll have hers too. "There, now we're all set."

"Cool."

After Eliza leaves, I decide to wait a little longer for the crowd to thin out. And for the remaining players, most of whom are doing on-ice interviews, to leave. It's then that I notice Nolan is one of the players being interviewed, though it looks like he's wrapping up. I can tell from the way he's leaning on his stick and shifting his weight from one skate to the other that he's itching to go.

When he's finally done with the sports reporter, he skates right by where I'm still seated. Clearly caught off guard by seeing me smack dab in the front row, especially with the game over, his eyes light up.

He gives me a nod, and I wave back. And then he breaks out into a genuinely happy grin. I know then that this is worth pursuing. This... this...whatever it is we're meant to be. But it can't be the same as before. I need to own this thing, take charge. No more letting Nolan set all the rules.

Suddenly, I know exactly what I need to do to make this work. What the new rules need to be.

I text Brent to let him know I have a ride home. I don't yet, but I plan to real soon.

After I leave the arena, I head straight to the players parking lot. The royal blue Mercedes SUV with the tinted windows, parked in a corner spot that should afford us privacy, belongs to Nolan.

When I try the passenger side door and find it unlocked, I let myself in.

"Should've locked your doors, Nolan," I murmur, "because now you're going to have to let me in to more than just your car."

9

FRIENDS? YEAH, I CAN DO THIS . . . MAYBE

NOLAN

Realizing Lainey is in my parked SUV fills me with a surprising sense of joy, like I felt when I saw her in the front row after the game. Even though I never expected her to be waiting for me out in the parking lot, I'm glad she is.

The truth is I've missed Lainey like crazy these past couple of weeks. I just couldn't bring myself to seek her out. I'm stubborn like that. But so is she, so she deserves a lot of credit for taking the initiative to put a stop to this stupid avoiding-each-other game we've been playing.

I open the back of the SUV and toss my gear inside, and then I go to the driver's side and gently slide in.

"Babe," I say real softly, not wanting to startle the crap out of her. "Hey, I'm really glad you're here. I know we need to finish the talk we started..." I trail off.

And then I have to suppress an outright laugh because, *how cute is this shit?* Lainey has fallen asleep in my car. With her head resting against the passenger side window, her hair is splayed across her cheek like a dark veil, making her look like a gorgeous angel.

"You really are incredibly beautiful," I whisper. Reaching over, I carefully brush shiny locks from her face. "Lainey..." I sound shaky. I'm feeling far more emotional than I expected.

Shit, this girl. She has me so twisted and turned half the time.

While I ponder why that is, she stirs. And then she's awake, but startled, grabbing my hand and bolting upright.

"N-Nolan?" she sputters. "What's going on?"

"I don't know," I say, laughing, my hand caught in her warm grasp and me liking it. "You tell me, seeing as you're the one sleeping in my car."

"Crap, you're right." She drops my hand. "I let myself in after I found the door unlocked. Which, incidentally..." Narrowing her eyes at me, she continues her admonishment. "...you should keep your vehicle locked at all times."

"Point taken. And thank you, Officer Lainey."

"I'm serious. Who knows what kind of lunatic might let themselves in!"

I raise a brow, and she waves me off. "Oh, shut up. I don't mean me. You know what I mean."

"I do," I concede, letting up.

She yawns then, and I notice she looks more tired than usual. "Have you been working a lot lately?"

"Yeah, I've been picking up a bunch of extra shifts and working tons of doubles."

"I was wondering why I haven't seen you around the neighborhood."

I throw that out casually, but I know the real reason and it has nothing to do with Lainey always working. Still, this'll move us along since I want to know why Lainey is in my vehicle.

My tactic works, as she then says, "Let's be honest here. Not running into each other has absolutely nothing to do with our work schedules."

I lean my head back against the rest. "Yeah, you're absolutely right."

When I glance over at her, she's brooding, chewing on her lower lip. Finally, she says, "We need to talk about what happened in my bedroom the night of Brent's party."

I straighten up, shake my head. I can't help it. Despite all the arguments I've run through in my head *and* my assertion that I'm ready to move forward, I'm clearly not. It's like some kind of fucking conditioned response, making it automatic for me to say, "If this is another 'Nolan, you need to make a commitment' speech—"

Lainey stops me in my tracks. "Hold it right there, buddy." Her eyes flash, her ire clear even in the dim lighting. "Not that this is that, but if it were why would it be so freaking horrible? What the hell happened in your past that was so damn terrible that you avoid these types of discussions like your life depends on it?"

"We're talking now, aren't we?" I snap.

She stares over at me, and then starts slowly shaking her head, like she can't believe my response. "I should just go," she says.

When she reaches for the door handle, I know I have to do something. She won't play this game forever. Nor do I want her to. It's just hard to break out of old habits. But I give it a try.

"You're right, Lainey. There is a reason why I get like this."

She sits back. "Go on."

I run my hand through my hair. "It's not that I don't *want* to tell you what the problem is, not anymore. It's just hard to actually put it into words."

"Well try."

"I am."

"No you're not. And I don't understand why that is. You were about to tell me everything in my bedroom that night."

"I was," I admit. "But it isn't that easy. To be honest, it doesn't feel like the right time anymore, and definitely not here."

It's bullshit. I'm deflecting.

Knowing that, Lainey fires back, "How is now any different than in my bedroom? Oh wait, I know. You haven't just finished fucking me."

I glare over at her. "That's not it and you know it."

I just can't do this. Not here, not like this, maybe not ever. I was wrong. I'm not fucking ready to talk about my failed marriage, my goddamn cheating wife, and all the humiliation I felt back then…and apparently still feel now.

"So why is now not a good time?" she presses.

There's no way she's getting jack out of me now, not in the middle of this argument.

"For one thing"—I wave my hand around—"we're in the middle of the goddamn players' parking lot."

Right, like location is the only thing holding me back.

Lainey sighs. "Whatever. Forget it. That's not why I came here to wait for you, anyway."

I look over at her and raise a brow. It's a dick thought, but I'm kind of hoping she wants sex, especially now. I could use a good release to jettison all the fucking crazy shit she's stirred up.

Lainey rolls her eyes. "I'm not here for that either, you perv."

"That's unfortunate."

Lainey ignores my smartass commentary and goes on, "Actually, though, sex *is* the reason why I got in your SUV tonight. Not to have it with you, but to talk about it with you."

"This should be interesting," I murmur cynically. "Sex talk with no sex."

We're going to *discuss* sex, as opposed to engage in it. Kind of a shame too, seeing as Lainey looks sexy as hell in the ripped jeans she's wearing. Her pale skin is peeking out the tears like a goddamn invitation to rip them some more. And that off-the-shoulder sweater is just screaming for me to pull it down and devour her luscious breasts.

"Nolan," she warns, noticing my hungry stare. "Behave."

"Okay, okay." I force my eyes up to her face. "Go ahead and start your little sex talk."

Now it's my turn to roll my eyes. She ignores me and goes on to inform me she's been thinking a lot lately—about us and what she wants from me. Turns out, it's pretty simple, and certainly not what I expected.

"Nothing," she says, throwing me for a loop. "I want nothing from you, Nolan. No commitment, no declarations of exclusivity, nothing at all."

"Huh?" To say I'm stunned would be an understatement. "What changed?"

I'm shocked, but hey, I can roll with this new development. No-strings sex with Lainey works for me. Maybe it's not happening tonight since we're only "talking" about it, but clearly easy sex is what this discussion is about, right?

I guess my sense of victory shows in my smug expression.

Lainey lets out a snort, and snipes, "You can wipe that *I won* smirk off your face right now, Nolan."

I school my features to something more neutral. "What smirk? I have no idea what you're talking about."

I kind of don't, seeing as it's Lainey who's wearing the smug expression now. And it just grows smugger and smugger, especially when she declares, "I came up with a solution. It's something that'll be good for both of us, as individuals and as a..." She waves her hand between us. "...whatever it is we are to one another."

"Okaaay." I'm more confused than ever. It doesn't happen often, except with this woman. She's the only one who has the ability to mess with my usual clear-headed thinking.

"So," she goes on, clearing her throat and letting me know things are about to get real serious here. "We both agree there's something between us, something more than sex, right?"

I concede, "Yes."

"But where you're at, and where I'm at—or rather where I *was* at—they're two totally different places."

"This is some fucked-up, confusing female logic," I mutter. "But yeah, I think I'm following."

"Good." She nods approvingly. "I've looked at it a hundred different ways, and I think the only chance for us to get beyond where we are now, where we're *stuck*, is to go ahead and start hanging out. Like, a lot."

"This doesn't sound too bad," I interject, and she gives me a look.

She then hits me with the bad part—"While we're doing all this hanging out, we have to agree to totally abstain from sex."

"What?" I wisely don't add what I'm really thinking, which is, *are you fucking crazy?*

"You heard me," Lainey says, oblivious to my horror at this new condition. "We need to step back and concentrate on being friends,

Nolan. And I mean *just* friends."

"Just friends, eh?" I roll it around in my mouth, and I don't like the way it tastes. "Friends with benefits would be much sweeter, Lainey." I cock a brow, along with a slice of my head her way.

She smacks my arm. "Be serious."

"Oh, Christ, I am being serious. But I have to tell you that I don't think I've *ever* been 'just friends' with any female, other than those in my family."

"Well see, this should be good for you."

"Good for me is a massage after a really physical game, or the team nutritionist giving me a new recipe for a kickass smoothie. No sex is *not* good for me, Lainey. Not in any way, shape, or form."

"You'll live," she dryly informs me.

"I may not," I maintain.

"Nolan, come on." She levels me with a look that says I better knock it the fuck off.

"Okay, okay." I raise my hands, capitulating to her crazy demand. "As of today, I vow to spend time with you as nothing more than…" I cough out the next part, "your friend."

Lainey puts her hand on my thigh. A friendly gesture, not a this-is-leading-to-something move.

"Ah, Nolan, don't look so sad. This'll benefit us both. We've never tried it this way. Ever since the night we met it's been sex, sex, and more sex."

"And that was bad?"

She glances away. "No. But we need something…different."

"Ahh, Lainey, you're going to be the death of me."

Since she's not yet moved her hand, I nod down, trying one final time to avoid the platonic curse of no-more-sex-with-Lainey.

"You sure you don't want me to fuck you one last time?" My voice is low, edged with the promise of the kind of raw sex I know she loves.

Releasing a stuttered breath, she yanks her hand from my thigh, like I just burned her.

"No, Nolan, absolutely not," she states emphatically. "I think you're missing the whole point here."

Despite her protests, I can tell she's weakening. "It's a definite no, then?"

"Yes. I mean no!" She literally growls in frustration. "What I'm saying is absolutely no sex, okay?"

Lainey's words, though loud, hold no conviction whatsoever, leading me to retort, "Like that sounded convincing."

"It doesn't matter." She looks away. "We need this. Otherwise, it's going to have to end."

"I don't want that to happen," I say softly.

"Okay." Her eyes meet mine as she confirms, "Then we agree to try it my way?"

I nod, acquiescing. "Okay, but what happens now?"

Pointing to the exit, she says, "Just drive us somewhere. Anywhere, I don't care. Just make sure it's someplace public. Maybe we could go to dinner. You're probably hungry, right?"

"Yeah, sure." I start up the SUV. "I can always eat." *Too bad I won't be eating her.*

I am hungry, as I always am after a game. More than that, I just want to spend time with this woman, even if she is off-limits…for now.

Shit, this is going to be tough.

But for her, I'm willing to try. And who knows? In the end, maybe she'll be right. Maybe something real and solid will emerge from this no-sex nonsense.

One can only hope.

10

DO THEY MAKE BURLAP SACKS IN SIZE FOUR?

LAINEY

Now that Nolan and I have decided to board the just-friends train, I no longer have to keep him a secret from my sister. She's still less than thrilled that we're planning on spending time together. She tells me she doesn't trust his intentions.

Ha!

Little does she know it's not only *his* intentions she needs to worry about. I may have come up with the "just friends" thing, but sticking with it promises to be a challenge for me too.

"We are talking about the same Nolan Solvenson, right?" Aubrey asks one afternoon when she, Brent, and I are out on the back patio, eating a picnic-style dinner.

I've just announced that my new bud Nolan and I are catching a movie this evening.

"Yes, the very one, Aubrey," I say, annoyed, as I scoop up another huge helping of potato salad from a large bowl at the center of the table. "I believe there's only one Nolan on the team."

"Thank God," Aubrey murmurs.

Brent chuckles, a little too in the know if you ask me. I don't think he's buying this friends-only crap for a minute.

Too bad for him, it's in play and, thus far, is working.

"I don't understand how you two became friends in the first place." Aubrey peers over at me from across the table, suspicious. "When did this little friendship start?"

"Yes, Lainey,"—Brent smirks—"when did the sudden closeness with Nolan begin?"

Schooling my face to a neutral expression, something I've picked up from Nolan, I reply, "I met him at his New Year's Eve party, remember?"

Brent, no doubt recalling my walk of shame the following morning, has the decency to lower his head and scratch the back of his neck. He may be a smartass, and he loves to pepper me with innuendo, but he's not one to tattle to Aubrey. Otherwise, I'd of heard about it.

But even without Brent busting me on spending the night at Nolan's that night, Aubrey has no trouble recalling the way we flirted with each other at the actual party.

"Wait," she says, "you and Nolan were all over each other on New Year's. That looked like a lot more than friendship, Lainey."

My sister isn't giving me a hard time to be a bitch. She ultimately has my best interest at heart. She doesn't want to see Nolan break my heart into a thousand I-told-you-so pieces.

But she needn't worry so much. "We're past that," I assure her. "We decided we work best as buds."

"If you say so, Lainey." Aubrey sighs. "I trust you know what you're doing."

Crap, I really hope I do too.

An hour later, and with that thought still jangling around in my mind, I walk the short distance to Nolan's house for our casual friends-only nondate.

I insisted he not pick me up, as it seemed more like what friends would do.

"You live close," I told him when we were working out the details. "I'll just bop on down to your place, and we can leave for the movie from there."

"Whatever, Lainey," he replied dryly, clearing humoring me.

When I reach his front door, I glance down and realize my blue spaghetti strap tank, even though it's layered under a blue and white checkered shirt, is revealing entirely too much cleavage.

My boobs are one of Nolan's weaknesses, so I quickly button up. When picking out clothes for this nondate, I chose jeans, Keds, and the shirt and tank ensemble, thinking it'd look fun and casual, but in no way sexy. Buttoned up, I'm good.

I ring the doorbell, feeling better about this whole thing and pretty sure it'll work.

But then Nolan answers, and I'm all like, "Whoa, wow." He clearly didn't receive the casual dress memo. He's decked out very date-like.

I narrow my eyes, wondering if he dressed so sharply on purpose to chip away at my resistance.

"Something wrong?" he asks, one brow arched.

Yes, something is wrong! The dark pants you're wearing and the crisp light-gray button-down make you him look like a freaking model, a very powerfully built model.

Wait, I can't tell him that. "No, nothing is wrong," I say, sighing. "You look nice, is all. I think I might be underdressed."

His eyes sweep over my body. "No, you look perfect, Lainey."

Our eyes meet, and just like that, a fire is ignited.

"This is going to be harder than we thought," he murmurs.

Why lie? "Yeah, it is," I agree.

"Well…" He rolls back his shoulders and steps away from the door. "Come on in, *friend.*"

I scurry past him, so as not to be tempted to touch his hard chest… or grab his wide shoulders…or kiss his chiseled face. In my haste, I get tripped up on my own two feet and almost do a header onto the foyer floor, which would really hurt like hell seeing as it is pure marble.

Nolan—hockey gods, bless his fast reflexes—catches me by an elbow and helps me right myself.

"Thanks," I murmur as I twist from his firm, manly grasp.

Those amazing hands have been all over my body. How can one innocent, protective and caring gesture have me so ready to cave?

Gesturing to the open door, and before I do something I'll regret, I blurt out, "We should go." I don't add, but definitely think, *before we end up in your bedroom.*

Blue eyes scan down my body appreciatively as he nods absently. Guess my buds-appropriate attire isn't quite enough to quell our passion. A burlap sack might be in order for our next nondate date.

"What is it?" I ask when his gaze lingers.

Chuckling, he says, "I was just thinking that you look really cute in that outfit."

"Nolan."

I pin him with a *don't go there* look. And he, well, he gets defensive.

"What's wrong with telling you that you look cute? It's just an opinion. Friends tell each other all the time when they think the other looks nice. I grew up with three older sisters, Lainey. I know the drill."

Nolan does come from a big family, three girls and two boys. He's the youngest of the crew. And though I've never met any of his siblings, I'd be willing to bet he's the one who thinks he knows it all, especially since he usually does.

I hear him chuckling as I scamper out the door.

As he's locking up behind us, he lets out a genuine laugh when he hears me muttering, "Wonder if they make burlap sacks in a size four."

11

WHAT HAPPENS IN VEGAS STAYS IN VEGAS

NOLAN

We can do this. Yes, we can. It's like hockey, all about discipline, which is something I have lots of.

Then again, maybe I don't when it comes to Lainey.

Touch me there. Oh God, yes, a little to the right. A female gasp, and then, *How have we stayed away from this?*

I don't know. But never again, baby. Never. If we make it through this night, I plan on touching you like this all the time.

A tasteful flash of boobs, two bodies rolling in the sheets.

No, it's not me and Lainey.

Unfortunately.

We're at the cinema, and I shift in my seat as I'm forced to watch two fucking actors get it on up on the big screen. And I do mean *fucking* actors, as in that's exactly what they're simulating, in rather explicit detail for a movie with an R rating. This movie is supposed to be a horror flick for God's sake!

Since we're on a roll with the fucking—fuck my life, this shit sucks.

I'm ready to throw in the towel on this "friends" bull, and go ahead and suggest to the girl next to me that we drop this charade and head back to my house to reenact what these two actors are pretending to do.

That's probably not a good idea, though.

Speaking of the girl next to me, she's elbowing me right now, hard, in the ribs.

"Ouch! What the hell is that for?" I ask when she continues to assault me.

Another sharp jab, I guess for good measure, then she says, "That's for picking out this movie, Nolan. What is wrong with you?" She doles out one more bony elbow shot. "You promised not to pick out a movie with sex in it."

"Hey, there was no mention of sex in the reviews I read," I say in my defense.

I'm confused, and more than a little dumbfounded, as to why there *is* a hot-as-hell love scene smack dab in the beginning of what's supposed to be a slasher flick.

I guess sex really does sell.

Carnal moaning blares from the huge speakers on the walls, and I suddenly hate surround sound. It makes everything *waaay* too realistic. The last thing two people trying to avoid ending up in bed, fucking each other's brains out, need to hear is *other* people doing exactly that.

Lainey starts squirming in her seat and angles herself as far away from me as she can, without actually getting up and moving to the empty seat next to her.

Yeah, this is affecting her too.

When a shot of the guy pumping away, going to town on the girl, pops up on the screen, Lainey jumps up and does indeed claim the empty seat.

I cock my head. "Is that really necessary?" I whisper over to her.

"Yes," she hisses back. But then she shoots me a *please understand* look.

I do understand—God, do I ever—so I give her a nod and whisper a resigned, "Okay."

Leaning over the empty seat, she assures me, "I'll come back and sit next to you once it's over."

"Great, but…" Shaking my head, I blurt out, louder than intended, what's going through my mind, "This is still so fucked up."

That last garners the attention of a much older man seated directly in front of me. He twists around to shush me.

"Sorry," I mutter.

Suddenly, his eyes widen, and slowly turning back to face the screen, I hear him say to the lady next to him, whom I assume is his wife, "I think that's Nolan Solvenson behind us. You know, honey, the hockey player."

Oh no. The last thing I need is to be recognized, seeing as my nondate "date" and I are acting so strangely—watching the movie with the seat between us unoccupied like we're a couple of teenage boys trying to be cool.

But of course, on this evening, one that's already weird as hell, things get even stranger when the silver-haired man turns back around and asks me to autograph his half-empty cardboard tub of popcorn.

I've signed odder things than this, so that's not an issue, but there is a problem. "Uh, I don't have a marker on me," I inform him.

Lainey, helpful girl that she is, returns to the seat next to me and starts digging around in her purse.

"Wait, I think I have one." Two seconds later, she pulls out a hot pink Sharpie and says, "Here you go."

She passes the marker to me, and I reply, "You're kidding, right?"

The autograph seeker's wife, who's now turned around and staring at me just as excitedly as her husband, assures me, "Pink is fine."

"Yes, yes, it is," the man adds, nodding fervently.

"I guess pink it is then."

Sighing, I sign my name…on a popcorn tub…in hot pink.

As I'm finishing up, a girl seated behind me reaches across to tap Lainey on the shoulder.

"Wow," she gushes, "you're out with Nolan Solvenson. What's it like to date a hockey player?"

Hello, I'm right here. She knows it. Oh, she sure does. Her arm is outstretched, touching Lainey, but rubbing up against my back.

I think she's doing it on purpose, to sort of backhandedly flirt. *Not happening, sweetheart.*

I clear my throat and turn to shoot her a look. The girl moves her arm. "Sorry," she says with a smile held with promise.

I roll my eyes at her, feeling bad for the dweeby dude she's with. He's watching the movie, acting like he can't see his girlfriend giving me googly eyes.

I ignore the girl and turn around so I can watch the movie, but she's right back to chatting it up with Lainey, whispering, "So what's it like, dating…?"

I assume she must be motioning to me, so I look over at Lainey to gauge her reaction. I'm curious how she plans to handle this little inquiry.

She starts out by stammering, "Oh, uh, I…" Her eyes dart from me to the girl.

Oh, hell. Swooping in to save the day, and to wrap this shit up before the other patrons start bitching about us talking, I wave around the pink marker still in my hand and say, "We're not dating. She's my—"

"Sister," Lainey blurts out.

She looks at me, and I look at her.

Shrugging, she informs Dweeby's date, "Yeah, I'm his younger sister."

Why she doesn't just tell the girl we're friends is beyond me. We're *trying* to be friends, right? Maybe Lainey feels this better explains our bizarre behavior during the now thankfully long-behind us sex scene.

I hand the popcorn tub back to the guy in front of me, and he takes it and thanks me. I then give Lainey back her marker, and everyone goes back to watching the movie. Thank God.

A few minutes later I go out to the concession stand, and Lainey and I then spend the next hour watching the movie and munching on buttered popcorn.

"This is actually a really well-done horror flick," she whispers to me about three-quarters of the way through. "But I'm glad the sex scenes are done."

I laugh and agree. "So I'm forgiven? Even though we did have to start off with a literal bang?"

That earns me another elbow to the side, albeit a gentle one. I'm beginning to think this elbowing business is Lainey's way of touching me without, you know, *touching* me.

"You are," she tells me. "But this is getting a little scary now, and I might not forgive you for that."

"Aw." I drape my arm around the back of her seat, careful not to touch her. "I may have picked a scary movie, but I'm here to protect you from the monsters on the screen."

"That's really sweet, Nolan," she murmurs, inching closer to me.

I'd like to put my arm around *her*, not just the seat. She's frightened, so she'd probably let me. But then again, she might move again. *Fuck.* The arm around the seat will have to do for now.

The movie plays on, and though I wouldn't characterize it as "scary," like Lainey thinks it is, it's definitely suspenseful. There are a lot of what-the-hell's-around-that-corner and don't-go-in-there-you-idiot moments.

To Lainey, though, it seems to be outright terrifying. I assume this because she continues to inch closer and closer to me. So much for the no touching. By the time we reach the climactic ending, she's snuggled against my shoulder and hiding her face in the crook of my neck.

Not that I'm complaining…or surprised. I remember Lainey once telling me that though she loves scary movies, she hates them as well. She *wants* to watch, but always ends up too scared to. She told me one time she hid behind her friend and just *listened* to the ending.

Shit, maybe that's why I chose this movie, like subconsciously. Maybe I was hoping Lainey would end up close to me, like she is now.

Oh hell, I go ahead and put my arm around her. Meanwhile, up on the screen the creepy clown-faced killer is breaking into a ramshackle cabin deep in the woods. The lead actress just went in the ramshackle building to hide.

Lainey looks up to watch, lets out a little squeak, and lifts the armrest between us. She moves so close she may as well just sit on my lap.

Covering her eyes with her hand, she whispers, "I don't know if I can watch the rest. I *want* to see what happens, but I just can't do it.

Can you tell me when the super scary part is over?"

"Ah, it's okay." I rub her back, chuckling. "It's only a movie," I remind her.

"I know." She peeks through her fingers to look up at me. "It's still freaking me out. I swear my heart's beating a mile a minute."

Her chest *is* heaving, though I shouldn't be staring, not there.

I tighten my arm around her shoulders. "Don't worry. I got you," I whisper into her hair.

"Thanks, Nolan."

Maybe holding her like this is comforting, seeing as, a minute later, she bravely announces, "Maybe I'll watch for a minute or two."

I look down at her, and say, "You should. I know you can do it."

I tighten my hold, and she smiles up at me. "Just don't stop holding me, okay?"

"Never."

God, she's so beautiful, vulnerable like this.

Resting her head on my shoulder, she finally turns her eyes to the screen. "I'm proud of you," I whisper.

She continues to watch, gripping my thigh in a death hold when the girl in the cabin finds a knife on the floor just as the killer is sneaking up on her.

The girl turns to face the killer, and Lainey squeaks out, "Nolan."

"You're good, babe." I kiss the top of her head. "I'm here."

I expect Lainey to close her eyes eventually, but she forges through, confronting her fears. In the movie, so does the girl. She charges ahead and stabs the villain, only enough to incapacitate him, though. The girl then runs out of the cabin, screaming for help, which arrives in the form of her love interest, the guy she was having the hot sex with in the beginning.

When the killer emerges from the cabin, as the psychos often do in these films, it's the love interest that saves her by shooting the bad guy. I realize then that even though this is a silly horror movie, I want to be that for Lainey. I want to be the man with whom she not only has the best sex of her life, but also the one she can always rely on to save her in the end.

I'd go up against a psycho killer for her any day, really I would.

But what the hell does that say about me and my feelings for her? Am I falling for Lainey Shelburne? Or have I already fallen, and that's why this "friends" act is killing me?

I continue to hold her as the credits start to roll, and she surprisingly lets me, even though she's no longer scared.

"I'm glad I watched the whole ending," she says softly, picking at a loose thread on my pants.

Her head is still on my shoulder so her face is really close to my neck. When she speaks her lips graze my skin, making me wish we were *not* friends.

"I couldn't have watched without you holding me," she says. "Despite all our issues, Nolan, I do feel safe when I'm with you. I shouldn't tell you this, but sometimes I feel like I could do pretty much anything with you by my side."

Shit, we are stepping way out of the friend-zone lines.

All I want to do is lean down and kiss the crap out of her. It would be so easy too, just this once. We could blame it on the movie, and then we could go back to the friend-zone. Though I have to say that zone is out of whack already, seeing how physically close we are right now.

Lainey looks up at me, her lips mere inches away.

"Babe," I murmur, my breaths mingling with hers.

"Nolan, I—"

Abruptly, she's cut off when the guy behind us—the dweeb—clears his throat very loudly.

That's weird…and rather rude.

It all becomes clear—at least it does to me—when I hear the girl next to him hiss, "Ugh! That is beyond disgusting!"

"Repulsive," he agrees. "Who would have ever thought that kind of shit goes on in professional sports?"

"Huh?" Lainey murmurs. "What the hell are they talking about?"

She settles back into her own seat, peering at me questioningly, like I know what's up the girl's ass.

Actually, I do. Thanks to Lainey telling the couple behind us that she and I are *siblings*, they now think we're into incest. After all, we were all mashed up in each other's business. Plus, we almost just *kissed*. Little wonder they're so freaked.

Lainey shoots the couple a dirty look, still not picking up on why they're so appalled.

When I start to chuckle, she wants to know, "What's so funny about rude people, Nolan?"

The couple continues to murmur in disgust as they stand and hasten to leave.

"That was just so weird," Lainey remarks once they're gone. And then, narrowing her eyes over at me, she says, "I still don't get how you can find this so amusing. That couple said some really rude things, for no good reason. We were nothing but nice to them."

I'm about to explain, but just then the older couple in the row in front of us gets up and turns around. They missed Lainey draped all over me, and we're seated normally now, so there are no distasteful comments or stares from them. I'm glad, since they seem nice and like genuine fans.

"Thanks again for signing this." The man raises his popcorn tub. "And good luck to you and the team this season."

I thank him, shake his hand, and he and his wife leave.

Lainey makes a face. "See, those two were fine," she says, still clearly bothered by the comments the other couple made. "I just don't get why those people behind us started acting so grossed out. What in the hell did we do?"

I can't let her remain in the dark another minute longer.

"Lainey, think about it. What did you tell that girl when she asked you about dating a hockey player?"

Suddenly, she gets it.

"Oh crap. I told her I was your sister."

"Yep." I nod.

We look at each other, and then we both lose it.

On our way out of the movie complex, we see the outraged couple standing by the exit doors. It's the only way out, so we have to head that way.

"Should we tell them the truth?" Lainey whispers as we near the exit.

"Nah, let's leave them fully immersed in their freak-out."

"Ooh, are you sure? 'Cause if you are, I have an even better idea."

Lainey shoots me a mischievous grin, and I say, "Uh-oh, what are you planning?"

She takes my hand. "Just roll with it, okay?"

"I can do that."

And I can, as I'm liking that her hand's in mine.

We start to pass the couple, and in a loud and crystal clear voice, Lainey says, "You are such a sweet *brother*. And so deliciously hot too. I hope Mom and Dad never figure out what we're up to because I don't think I could ever stop."

The couple gasps, and Lainey winks at them.

And then she says to the twosome, "Isn't it great that what happens in Vegas stays in Vegas?"

She drops my hand and grabs my ass, and the couple scurries off like the place is on fire.

Fuck me. Even though this is all for show, I swear in that moment I fall a little harder for my pretend "sister" and real-life "friend."

THE TRUTH, AT LAST

LAINEY

Nolan and I leave the poor couple, probably damaged for life, scurrying across the cineplex parking lot to get as far away from us as they can. We can't help but laugh all the way to his SUV.

"You are twisted, but I love it," Nolan tells me.

"I'm sure they'll figure it out," I reply.

He nods. "Yeah, all they have to do is look up my bio. They'll see all my sisters are way older. And none of them look like you."

"It was fun though, right?"

"It sure was."

I look over at him as we approach his vehicle. I can tell he'd like to put his arm around me again, or even maybe hold my hand. But now that we're out of sight of the couple, all touching has stopped. We're back to being reserved around each other. With no scary movie as an excuse to get close, and no more gawking couples to shock, we have no choice but to behave.

I shouldn't have grabbed his ass, it makes behaving now a challenge. His glutes felt so solid, reminding me of how they feel sans pants—or, better still, when I reach down and feel his firm ass as he pounds into me.

We start home, and I watch him surreptitiously as he drives us to our separate houses. At one point I let out a little sigh, thinking, *why must he exude sex all the time?* Like now, as the muscles in his powerful legs bunch up under his dark pants when he shifts gears. God, I love how strong hockey players' lower bodies are. Come to think of it, their upper bodies are pretty amazing too.

"Are you all right?" Nolan asks when I let out another long sigh.

"Yes," I reply.

But I'm not, not really.

He glances over at me when he comes to a stop sign. We share a look that says, *this is how it has to be.*

Nolan resumes focusing on the road as he starts moving again, but now it's his turn to sigh.

Okay, enough awkwardness!

"So," I begin, clearing my throat, "that movie was pretty good, especially that ending."

Hey, I'm proud I watched it. I need to reiterate my views.

"Yeah, it was pretty decent," he agrees. "Way better than I expected."

We reach our gated community, and Nolan turns in. As he drives through the myriad of palm tree-lined roads, the glow from the streetlamps bathes his strong, chiseled profile in a sultry amber shade.

I sigh again, and out of the blue, I guess to make conversation, he says, "Just how much of the whole movie did you actually see, Miss Hide Your Face on my Shoulder?"

"I saw most of it, especially after—" I search for words not laden with relationship innuendo, but can't find any, so I go with the truth. "—you made me feel safe enough to open my eyes. I watched every second after that."

Smiling over at me, he says softly, "I'm glad I make you feel safe."

"You know why that is, right?"

He shakes his head.

"It's because I trust you, Nolan."

I do. Not always in affairs of the heart, but when it comes to trust in general I know he has my back.

We reach Brent and Aubrey's house just then, and he pulls up to the curb, looking a little tense. We both know there's more we need to say, but not if Brent or Aubrey are around.

When Nolan sees we're good, his shoulders relax. Running a hand down his face, he says, "I'm glad you trust me, Lainey. But I know it's not in every way."

I know where he's going with this, and I'm quick to maintain, "Nolan, we *need* to do this friendship thing."

"I know, I know." He releases a pent-up breath. "I just hope someday I can earn your trust in *everything*."

"What about me? Do *you* trust *me*?"

"Yes, I do."

"Then finish telling me what you started to say that night in my bedroom. Tell me why you are the way you are, why you're so against committing to someone." I don't add, *like me*.

"Lainey." His voice hints at irritation, like a warning to back off. But I can't do that, not anymore. I'm taking a stand, taking charge, like

I've done with the friendship thing.

"We're friends now, Nolan," I state firmly. "And friends tell each other things."

"I don't," he snaps.

"Yes, you do," I counter. "You shared your big secret with Brent, right? Don't even try to deny it. Aubrey told me you did."

He rolls his eyes upon hearing that disclosure. "I swear, your sister…"

"I'm not anywhere close to being done," I warn, "so don't change the subject. I'm not here to talk about Aubrey."

"Oh, come on, Lainey."

"Seriously, what could be so damn awful that you can't just tell me? What happened to you? Was it a woman? Did she do you wrong?"

I look over at him, and his lips are pressed together so firmly that I know I'm on the right track. I have to say, Nolan frazzled is quite a sight.

"I want to know," I whisper, since I'm sensing he's close to breaking and opening up. "There's never going to be a perfect time. Just tell me this freaking secret so we can quit going around in circles."

"You really don't want to know," he murmurs.

"Yes. Yes, I do."

Leaning his head back against the rest, he coughs out a humorless laugh. When it's clear he's actually *not* going to say anything more on the subject unless I push it, I let my frustration be known.

"What the hell?" I throw up my hands. "Are you hiding some secret love child or something?"

That makes him laugh. "No, it's nothing like that."

"Were you once in prison?"

"Hardly," he scoffs.

"Okay, you had a drug problem then?"

"Nope, that was never my scene."

"Well," I continue, almost out of ideas, "what could it be? It's not like you were married once or something."

Silence.

Oh, shit. "Nolan?"

He stares out the side window, his face averted so I can't see his expression. But still, I know right then and there that I just hit the freaking nail on the head.

"You were, weren't you?" I say softly. "You were married once."

"Yes," he replies, the *s* trailing off, making him sound sad. Not sad as in wanting his marriage back, but sad as in he failed. "It was a long, long time ago, Lainey."

Wow, I never expected this. "You're only twenty-six. How long ago could it have been?"

"Many years ago," he replies. "I was barely eighteen at the time, and so was she. It didn't last long, only a couple of months."

Quietly, so as not to spook this very private man who's finally opening up to me, I say, "Can I ask what happened?"

He tells me everything then, how he was young and naïve and thought he was madly in love.

"I was a *much* more trusting person back then," he says.

I scoff, and he lets out a chuckle. "Hard to believe, I know."

"It is a little tough to imagine," I admit.

"I was very different from how I am now."

We look at each other, and I know he's thinking the same as me—that it's sad when part of your heart dies.

"Anyway," he goes on, looking away, "she took advantage of all that misplaced trust. She cheated on me with so many fucking men it was almost laughable. My teammates at the time were fair game for her, strangers too. Pretty much anyone with a cock, she set her sights on him."

"How has any of this never come out?" I marvel, amazed that it hasn't.

He explains. "At the time I'd been picked up by an NHL team, but was sent down to their minors system. This woman who became my wife was with me through all that. She kept telling me she was sure I was good enough that I'd get called back up soon, and every time she'd say that she'd push for us to get married."

"She wanted a hockey player husband?"

"Very much."

"So what happened?"

"I wanted to wait, but then…she told me she was pregnant."

I feel sick. "Oh, God. What happened to the baby, Nolan?"

"There never was any baby. I found out later that she said that just to get me to commit. It worked too. We went the next day to the courthouse and got married. She didn't care there was no fanfare. She'd landed herself a professional hockey player, and that was all that mattered. Only problem was she didn't really love me."

"Oh, Nolan…" I want to reach out to him, but I'm afraid, so I simply say, "I'm sorry."

"Don't be," he says on a sigh. "I was just so stupid back then. I believed she really loved me, even after she tricked me into marrying her. We didn't socialize much, so no one knew we'd gotten married. *She* wanted it that way, claiming it was because maybe someday we'd want a big, fancy wedding, where we could invite everyone we knew. She'd say 'why ruin it for everyone by telling them we're already married.'"

He pauses to scrub his hands down his face, and though it was long ago, it's clear this still hurts him.

"I later realized her wanting to keep the marriage quiet was only so she could pretend she was just some casual girlfriend of mine and thereby fuck my teammates."

"I don't even know what to say. That's just horrible and disgusting."

"It is," he agrees. "The code is wives are usually off-limits. But girlfriends, especially casual ones, are fair game. She knew that."

I've wanted to reach for him, and now I finally do. He lets me, and I lace my hand with his.

"Do you want to know how I found out what she was up to?" he asks, after a long pause.

I'm not sure I do, but it seems he wants to tell me. It's like now that his story is out he *has* to share it to completion, so I whisper, "Okay."

He squeezes my hand. "Fuck, Lainey, I couldn't have been more naïve. So this one night, we go out drinking with some real goon that was down in the minors with me. I'm drunk as hell and the three of us end up back at our crappy little apartment. The room's spinning so I lie down on the sofa. But before I pass out, my wife tells me she'll see my teammate out and that she's then going up to bed. I think nothing of it, trusting her completely. A little while later, I wake up because there's fucking water dripping on my head."

I give him a confused look, but I don't think he sees. But he does continue his story…

"It was just a drop every minute or so, but by the time it woke me up my hair and that whole side of the sofa was soaking wet. I figured there must be a leak, seeing as the bathroom was right above me. I thought, 'hey, I better go check it out.' So I dragged my still-drunk ass up the stairs and down the hallway to the bathroom. And that's when I heard giggling coming from the other side of the closed door."

I squeeze his hand to let him know I'm here, and he gives me a sad smile.

"The door wasn't even locked. I walked right in on that goon fucking my wife. He had her bent over the sink and was nailing her so hard that they'd dislodged the pipe going into the wall. That's why water was dripping down on my head. It was leaking right through the bathroom floor and down through the living room ceiling."

This is so, so bad. "Did you beat the hell out of the guy?" I ask.

He shakes his head slowly. "Why bother? Their backs were turned and they hadn't even noticed me. I left the apartment that night and never went back. I started divorce proceedings the next day. And that's when I vowed I'd never again allow myself to be put in that position."

"So you said 'fuck love,'" I murmur, understanding him a little better.

"I did," he whispers.

His story is awful and humiliating, and I understand why he's strived to keep it a secret. I'd want to hide something like that too.

"Where's your wife now?" I ask.

"Ex-wife," he corrects. And then he says, "Why do you want to know?"

I let out a snort. "I was thinking if she's not too far away, maybe I can go kick her ass for you."

That gets him to smile. "You'd have to take a couple of flights, I'm afraid. That goon she was messing around with…"

"Yeah?"

"He's from Austria. He never made it out of the minors, and I heard he moved back there a few years ago. Guess who went with him?"

My eyes widen. "Your ex?"

"Yep, and they're supposedly married now."

"Nolan, I—I just don't know what to say."

"You don't have to say anything, Lainey. Like I said, it was a long time ago."

But it's still affecting you, I want to say.

Instead, I go with "I'm sorry you were hurt. You were a young man with a trusting heart. And you're still that same man in a lot of ways."

"Not in the slightest." He laughs bitterly. "I don't trust anyone now."

"That's sad, Nolan."

"Sad, but true."

After a long pause, I say, "For the record, I'd never do anything like that to you."

"I'd never give you a chance."

"Wow, that's harsh."

"It is what it is, Lainey."

"And therein lies our problem," I snap.

I'm hurt by his absolute conviction to never again open himself up to the possibility of getting hurt, and I tell him as much.

When he rolls his eyes at me, I say, "That's exactly why we're in the friend-zone, Nolan."

I'm more determined than ever now not to give in and sleep with him. If I do, nothing will ever change. He clearly has a long way to go to get past this level of hurt.

When he doesn't rebut what I've just said, I add resignedly, "We made the right decision to just be friends."

He gives me a curt nod. "You're probably right."

Reaching for the door handle, I murmur, "I should go."

"Yeah, okay. We can talk tomorrow or something."

I nod and step out of the SUV, feeling more dismayed than ever.

Sometimes we want the truth so badly. But often, once we get it, instead of making things more clear things are left more muddled than ever.

COACH T WILL HAVE MY ASS IF THAT HAPPENS

NOLAN

The regular season begins.

My schedule is full, but I make time to hang with Lainey. Now that she knows the truth, she's more careful than ever to keep me at arm's length—physically, that is. Emotionally, it's a different story. We become closer than ever. With no relationship pressure in the way, we start to become actual friends. And I really love it.

I find I can talk to her about a lot of stuff—shit that goes down with the team, worries I have when I go into a scoring slump the first couple of games, and a lot of other random crap.

After going a third game without a single point, it's Lainey who assures me that everything will be all right.

And it is. The next game I score a goal and rack up two assists.

I feel so relaxed around her these days. She never pushes anything.

And apart from the incident at the cinema, she's controlled around me. There's no more crawling into my lap, no more lips almost brushing. It's like now that she knows my secret, she's backed way the fuck off.

I guess I have too, which is good in some ways, and bad in others.

It's good that I'm behaving, since I know I could hurt her if we stepped over that line. But it's bad in the sense that it makes her so much more of a challenge for me. And hell, I fucking thrive on challenges. I want so badly to chase her, as doing so calls to my competitive nature. *That's* why I must keep things in check.

Or at least try.

But it's really hard when she comes over to my house wearing short-shorts like she's prone to do. She looks hot pretty much all the time, adding to the challenge. And I swear to every hockey god up there that if she wears that damn sex-me-up cocktail waitress outfit in my presence one more time, I will *not* be held responsible for my actions.

I better get my shit together, though, and fast. I hear her coming in downstairs. Yeah, I gave her a key to my house. Just so she can water my houseplants when the team's on the road. Or that's what I told her. Too bad the only houseplants I have are cacti, which don't require all that much water.

"They still need love," I remind myself, chuckling as I step out of the upstairs shower. Shit, I realize then maybe it's *me* I'm talking about.

Dismissing that possibility as fast as I can, I grab a towel off the bar and gingerly wrap it around my waist. Stepping out into the hall, I yell down over the balcony rail, "Hey, Lainey, give me about five minutes to get dressed. Practice ran a little later than usual this morning. Coach T had us doing drills for an extra half hour, that fucker!"

I expect her to laugh, but I only get a distracted, "No problem."

Hmm, wonder what has her attention so diverted?

Too bad I don't have to time to figure it out. I need to hurry. Lainey and I have lunch plans this afternoon, but not just for the two of us. We're meeting her new friend, Eliza, at a chic new café. I guess Lainey's been hitting it off with the girl really well. They've gone shopping together once or twice and went out to dinner the other night. Anyway, she wants me to meet her.

New friend Eliza also happens to be Coach T's daughter, the one he keeps far from us. This should be interesting, especially since Benny's joining us. This morning after practice I invited him, simply because I don't want to listen to girl-talk the whole time. He was more than up for joining in. I think it's because he's curious to see what Coach's daughter is like. And, well, what she looks like, as well. A few of the guys who've seen her around claim she's a sexy little thing.

I'm still standing in the hall and I need to move my ass, so I turn around to head back to the bedroom to get ready. But then I hear Lainey sighing wistfully. This and her distracted response a moment ago make me wonder what's up, so I glance down to where she's waiting.

Aah, now I see, I think smugly.

Lainey's eyes are what're up. As in, she has a perfect view up under my towel from where she's standing in the foyer. She's taking me *all* in too, staring hungrily at my junk as she absently chews at her bottom lip.

I clear my throat, and she looks away swiftly. "See something you like?" I can't help but ask.

I'm teasing, but kind of not.

I know I'm venturing into possibly dangerous territory, but it feels like forever since she and I have just straight-up flirted, probably not since movie night.

Oh, what the hell. I'm standing here in nothing but a towel, so I may as well have some fun with it.

"'Cause Lord knows," I go on, "that I sure see something *I* like. You know what that outfit does to me, Lainey."

Yep, you guessed it—she has on that damn bar wench uniform that drives me insane. I can't help but sweep my gaze lustfully over her body. Told you I couldn't be held responsible for my actions if she wore those damn clothes again in my presence.

"I have a shift after lunch," she says by way of explanation. "I had to wear this. I won't have time to drive back and change."

"Uh-huh, okay." I can't tear my eyes away from her.

"Nolan…" She focuses solely on my face, though it seems to take all her effort to do so. "You know we can't do this."

I close my eyes, swallow hard. She's right. "I know, and I'm sorry. I shouldn't have said those things."

"Well, I shouldn't have been, you know, staring up your towel like that. I mean, I knew it was wrong. But in my defense, Nolan, so much of you is just so"—she waves her hand around, indicating my cock, which is still hanging in the breeze—"out there for all to see."

I step away from the rail. "I better get dressed."

"Good idea."

An hour later, lunch has concluded and the four of us are still at the café, just shooting the breeze. I look around the table and think, *I'm glad we did this.* Lunch was great, but this post-lunch relaxing is even better. Apart from one little thing—Benny and Eliza seem to be hitting it off a little *too* well.

Coach T will have my ass if anything happens between them. I invited Benny today, so it'd fall on me.

Fuck.

"Dude, did you even hear one word of what I was just saying?" Benny asks, turning to me.

All eyes are on me. *Great.* I have no idea what I just missed.

Lainey places her hand on my forearm. I'd rather see that warm little hand placed somewhere else on my body… But—wait, no.

Shit, I'm losing it today.

"You okay?" she asks me.

I shake my head, not to say *no,* but to clear my mind.

"Yeah, I'm fine," I say at last. "I was just lost in thought over something."

I don't add that I'm thinking how Coach Townsend will probably have *all* our heads if Benny ever bangs Eliza. He works hard to keep his daughter far removed from us players, pretty much for that exact reason. He also happens to be fully aware of Benny's extensive womanizing habits. He'd go ballistic if those two ever hooked up.

"Solvenson?" Benny prompts.

I still have no idea what's going on, so I ask, "Uh, what are we talking about again?"

Benny gives me a look, like *what's up with you, man,* but he lets it go and fills me in. "I was just telling the girls that I think they should come to our game tonight."

Oh, thank God it's nothing major. "Yeah, sure." I shrug. "If they're up for it, I think that's a great idea."

"I'd love to go," Eliza chimes in enthusiastically as she turns a flirty smile Benny's way.

I mentally roll my eyes.

"My shift's done at seven," Lainey then informs us. To Eliza, she says, "I can meet you inside the arena after work."

"That sounds great," Eliza responds.

This time when she smiles over at Benny, he grins back just as wide.

Ah, hell to the no.

Lainey looks at them and smiles approvingly. That's no help. Looks like it's on me to do whatever I can to keep my friend and the coach's daughter from making the biggest mistakes of their lives.

MATCHMAKING ME

LAINEY

The Wolves are playing the Washington Capitals. When I meet up with Eliza just inside the arena entrance, it's shortly before the game is set to start.

I'm smiling even before I reach her. This is my kind of girl! Not because she's wearing cute skinny jeans, a regulation black and red Wolves jersey, and a Wolves hair tie in her strawberry blonde hair, all of which I'd have worn had I had time to change. But no, that's not why I'm grinning. I'm laughing inside because Eliza has some huge-ass girl nads. She's standing there, blatantly twirling around a sparkly, red, white and blue Capitals-themed wristlet in her hand.

"Are you crazy?" I say when I reach her. Nodding down to her little bag, I add, "You do know that's the opposing team tonight, right?"

She laughs. "Yeah, I know."

"Well, it's mighty brave of you to bring it in here with these crazy fans." Just as I finish, some guy walks by and snorts as he peers down at the purse.

Eliza gives him the middle finger, thankfully as he's walking away.

As if she hasn't caught on yet, I still feel compelled to inform her, "Ever since winning the Stanley Cup, the Wolves fans have turned into home team fanatics."

She leans in close and whispers, "I know. I like to live dangerously."

"Clearly," I scoff.

Just then a female fan walks by and, nodding to Eliza's clutch, obnoxiously states, "Ovechkin sucks."

"He does not!" Eliza yells as the girl hurries off.

She starts to follow her, until I grab her arm and steer her away. "What are you doing? Think how embarrassing it'd be if you got into a fight."

Eliza is quite the little spitfire.

"Yeah," she sighs. "I guess you're right. My dad would have a fit."

Gesturing to her Caps wristlet, I ask, "Speaking of your dad, does he even know you own that thing?"

"He does." She smiles mischievously. "And he hates it *so* much. But it's really all his fault."

"What do you mean?"

"It was his idea for me to go to Georgetown. He should've foreseen me becoming at least a little bit of a Caps fan after three years in DC, right?"

She does have a point. Though, for tonight, I suggest she keep the wristlet out of sight.

"I think I will," she finally concedes when a guy walks by and sneers at her. "I'll keep it tucked up in the sleeve of my jersey."

She makes a show of slipping her little bag up under the gaping cuff of her too-large-for-her shirt, and I say, "That's better. Now you look like a full-on Wolves fan."

"Yep, I'm game-ready."

I peer down at my own outfit then. Crap, I don't look game ready *at all*. There was no time to change after work—not that I had clothes with me anyway. But I can fix that now.

Glancing around at the numerous team apparel shops in the concourse, I say, "Maybe I should buy a jersey too. Not only would I fit in better with the crowd, but I'm feeling a little like a hockey hooker looking for some action wearing this getup outside of work."

It's true. I've received quite a few looks already. Not angry stares like Eliza was getting for the wristlet, but leering, pervy looks. *Yuk.*

Eliza's purses her lips together and skims her gaze over my body, nodding like she understands my conundrum, especially when she reaches my substantial cleavage. "Yeah, maybe we better hit the stores."

"That's what I thought."

I lace my arm with hers and we go into a shop called Fan Stop. After I sort through a bunch of player jerseys, I settle on a Solvenson one. Like there's any other choice for me. My soon-to-be purchase is black and red, with the number seventy-seven on the front, back, and sleeves. It's oversized, even more so than Eliza's. I don't mind since it'll kind of be like having Nolan all over me.

Nolan...all...over...me. *Gah!*

Better think of something else, anything else. So I do. It's a random thing, and I end up repeating it to Eliza. "Did you know Nolan calls these things 'sweaters,' never 'jerseys.'"

"Huh." She nods thoughtfully as we reach the register, where the sales girl starts ringing me up. "My friend from Ottawa calls them that too. It must be a Canada-thing."

"Guess so," I say.

I ask the girl at the register to cut off the tags before we leave. Once that's done, I inform her I won't need a bag. I tug the jersey—or is it sweater?—over my head and adjust it till the bottom edge completely covers the short hemline of my black skirt.

"Hmm…"

I twist up my face, and Eliza asks, "What now?"

"I don't know. This new look might be worse than the work outfit by itself."

"How's that?"

"Now it looks like I'm wearing nothing but the jersey."

"Aw, don't worry about it," Eliza urges.

"Great," I murmur. "So now my choices are look like a hockey hooker or look like a puck bunny looking for some action."

"Oh, stop. You look really hot, and that's a good thing. Just own it."

That's sweet of her to say, but from the looks I'm receiving as we're leaving the store, I just don't know. I decide to do like she said and just own it.

"Yeah, it doesn't matter," I declare, all *I am woman, hear me roar.* "Let them look and think what they want. I'm here to enjoy the game."

"That's the spirit," Eliza says. "Now let's go find our seats."

We soon discover we're in the same section as we were for the preseason game, the night Eliza and I met. Only this time we're not in the front row, we're three rows back.

"I actually kind of like these seats better," I say to her once we get situated. I don't add that it's because I'll have a better view of Nolan, even when he's on the other side of the ice.

"They are nicer," she agrees. "I can see more of the ice."

Our team comes out then for pregame warm-ups. Eliza leans forward and starts searching the players.

I wonder if she's looking for Benny.

Yep, she is. It's pretty obvious from the way she smiles and waves to him when he takes the ice with Nolan. He gives Eliza a nod, so I do the same to Nolan. He's skating by and smiles up at me. *Wow, he looks amazing tonight.* There's just something about him, an extra jump in his step or something.

Wow, is there ever, I'm thinking a minute later.

Nolan is on fire as he starts taking practice shots at the goal manned by our goaltender, Ruslan "Breeze" Brezzenov. I guess now that Nolan's sloughed off his little scoring slump, which I assured him wouldn't last, he's feeling über confident.

And he has every reason to. Three slapshots and a wrister get by Breeze, who curses him out, albeit in a good-natured manner. Nolan laughs at his net minder flipping out. Benny skates over and says something that makes Nolan laugh even harder. He's always stunning, but especially so when he's in a really good mood, like he seems to be right now.

I just can't help myself—Nolan's smile makes *me* smile. But then I have to let out a resigned sigh. Too bad we're relegated to the friend zone. I know it's necessary for the time being, but it's not like I revel in it.

Eliza starts asking questions about Benny, and I welcome the distraction.

"Do you know if he's seeing anyone?" she asks, her eyes glued to the guy as he takes off his helmet over by the bench, letting his longish, dark blond hair flow, in order to adjust a strap.

I tell her, "I'm pretty sure he's not." But in the interest of full disclosure, and because I like Eliza and don't want her to ever be deluded that Benny is something he's not, I say, "I've heard he's a player, though. And I don't mean just on the ice."

"Hmm…" Armed with this new info, she still can't tear her gaze from him. Wow, she's really into him.

"Maybe he is," she continues dreamily. "But I've always believed that when a man finds the right woman, he can change those man-whoring ways pretty quickly."

I raise a brow. "Does that mean you're interested in him, like, for real for real?"

"Maybe." She shrugs. "We'll see."

All righty then. I guess we will.

I can't imagine Coach T will welcome this development, but then again the heart wants what the heart wants. Who is he to stand in the way of love? And really, who is anyone to? Certainly not me.

I resolve then and there to do whatever I can to help Benny and Eliza get together. I saw the way he looked at her at lunch this afternoon. It was obvious he likes her too.

Wow, maybe they'll even end up falling in love! That'd be amazing. Just because I can't have love doesn't mean my friends shouldn't have a shot at everlasting happiness. Or even just the temporary kind.

With visions of how matchmaking may aid me in not thinking so much about my own nonexistent love life, the game gets underway. The Caps score early, but Dylan Culderway, one of our top defensemen, scores from the point on a power play with only 1:18 left in the first period.

Midway through the next twenty minutes, Eliza grabs my arm excitedly when Benny puts up an assist on a beautiful goal from Nolan. "Wow, that was a nice one," she says excitedly.

"It was," I agree as I watch the replay on the Jumbotron. Benny and Nolan, fast skaters that they are, created a two-on-one situation during a Caps change. And, no pun intended, they quickly capitalized on it.

The game gets even more exciting during the third period. Nolan scores a goal ten seconds in and the crowd goes crazy. And then, a short while later, a little shiver runs down my spine when Nolan scores what ends up being his first hat trick of the season.

Ballcaps rain down on the ice and all I can think is, *wow, all this energy for Nolan.* I can literally feel the enthusiasm of the fans. I wish I could share my own enthusiasm with Nolan after the game, in one very specific way.

Damn it, this friends thing is getting trickier and trickier as the weeks go by. Shouldn't it be getting easier? When are we going to fall into a comfortable routine? When will my insane attraction to him start to wane?

A little voice inside my head whispers, *never.*

Thankfully, Eliza pulls my attention from all these confusing questions when she leans in and says, "Wow, this is awesome. I wish I'd worn a hat."

"Yeah," I agree. "I wish I'd thought ahead and bought one down in the shop when I got the jersey."

I try to get Nolan's attention since he's on this side of the ice, but he's too busy celebrating with his teammates. There's a break afterward to clear all the hats, and then the game resumes.

There's no more scoring, and the Wolves end up winning the game.

Now it's time for someone, meaning Eliza, to win in the game of love. Before we leave, I ask her if she's up for going back to the family lounge and finding out what Nolan and Benny plan on doing once they're showered and changed.

"Maybe we could all go out and grab a bite to eat," I throw out, shrugging.

Step one in my matchmaking plan is underway.

Eliza's springtime-green eyes light up. "I'm up for that," she tells me.

"You're not worried about your dad seeing you back there?" I raise a brow.

"Nope. I found out he leaves by a different door. He'll never see me."

"Sneaky girl, I love it." I take out my phone, laughing. "The guys should be in the locker room by now." I enter my password to unlock the phone. "I'll just text Nolan now and give him the heads-up on where we'll be. I'll ask if he *and Benny*"—I give her a conspiratorial wink—"want to go grab a late dinner."

"Sounds perfect," she replies, smiling wide.

I compose my text, typing in what I just told Eliza, and then I hit *Send*.

I'm giddy at the prospect of some good old-fashioned matchmaking. But my hopes are dashed when Nolan texts back that he *and* Benny, plus a couple of other guys, already have plans to go out.

Is it okay if we join you? I text back.

Uh, not tonight, he replies. *We'll just plan something for another time, okay?*

It's kind of not okay. This feels like a blow-off.

Shoving my phone back in my purse, I give Eliza the bad news and finish up with, "That was really weird."

"In what way?"

"Nolan just seemed so abrupt. Whatever." I shrug. "I just thought it was rude that he made it crystal clear we're not invited to *wherever* it is they're going."

Eliza taps a finger to her chin. "Hmm, I bet I know where they're heading."

"Oh yeah, where's that?"

"To that new gentlemen's club that recently opened. It's just down the road." When I look confused, she says, "Haven't you heard about it? Apparently it's very high-end and strictly men-only."

"How do you know all this?" I ask. "I haven't heard a single thing about any gentlemen's club."

Of course Nolan would never share information on a new strip club with me. He knows I hate that he's into strippers. Not that I've seen any evidence he's been to any clubs recently. But old habits die hard.

I ask Eliza then to tell me everything she knows. She goes on to inform me, "I overheard my dad bitching about the place the other day. He was talking on the phone with someone, and he said the last thing his players needed was a distraction three short blocks from the arena."

"A gentlemen's club…" I let out a sarcastic cough. "They may as well just call it what it is—a disgusting strip joint!"

"Really." Eliza rolls her eyes.

I then get to thinking, which is always dangerous, especially when that interview Nolan did with Marty Quick keeps popping into my mind. Visions of Nolan and hordes of strippers crowd my thoughts, like a thong-clad army. All I know is I don't like this. Nolan's been sexually frustrated because he can't have me. What kind of trouble might he get into if he's inundated with strippers at this club?

Possibly a lot of trouble, with many naked female bodies, like he did in Toronto, over the course of two days, with nine freaking strippers!

No. Just hell no!

"I know what we need to do," I say to Eliza.

"What?"

"We need to pay this little men-only club a visit."

"Why?"

I can't tell her about Nolan's indiscretion, or about how I'm feeling the need to get my ass down there to keep him from making the same mistake he did this past summer. So I just say, "Don't you think it'd be funny if we got in somehow? Imagine the looks on Nolan and Benny's faces when they see *us* in their little den of iniquity."

"Yeah, that could be kind of fun," she agrees. "Surprising them like that."

I sense she's really just looking for a way to see Benny again. But hey, that works for me.

After a beat, she asks, "How do you suppose we'll get in? It's men-only, remember?"

"Ah, I actually think I have a way around that."

I go on to share my ingenious plan with Eliza, stressing again how fun it'll be to turn the tables on the guys. I don't add that this is more about my attempt to keep Nolan far, far away from the talent.

I JUST CAN'T STAY AWAY FROM TITS AND ASS

NOLAN

I just can't stay away from tits and ass, though tonight I have a good reason.

In the interest of keeping my friend and linemate safe from the wrath of Coach T, which is necessary when I receive the text from Lainey asking if Benny and I would like to join her and Eliza to go eat somewhere, I nominate him and myself to join the couple of players planning on checking out some new gentlemen's club down the street.

Since I don't really want to go, and misery loves company, I get to work on trying to enlist Brent to join me and Benny and the two other dudes.

"Hey, man," I say to him when he steps out of the showers, towel around his waist. "How about escaping Aubrey's clutches for a while tonight? We're heading down to that new strip club."

It's no surprise when Brent sits down on the bench by his locker and says, "Thanks for asking, but I think I'll pass."

"Your loss, man," Benny interjects as he's straightening his tie. He's farther along in the getting-ready department since he didn't have as many post-game interviews as Brent and I did.

Which incidentally, man, what a great game.

"Boys," Brent says, his tone putting the kibosh on any motivation for pressing him to join us. "I got everything I could ever want, or need, waiting for me back at my house."

I resist the urge to gag. But then again, does the idea of a committed relationship like Brent and Aubrey's really make me feel sick?

Not so much anymore.

The old Nolan would be calling out Brent, saying he's a pussy. But this new version of me is content with keeping my mouth shut and accepting his response with grace. Truth is, when you get right down to it, I don't really want to go to this strip joint either. I'm doing it solely to keep Benny and Eliza from making a fucking major mistake.

Seems my taste for strippers and strip clubs has waned considerably since spending so much time with Lainey. We label ourselves "just friends," but some stupid, hopeful part of me is waiting for her to give the green light for us to move forward and get back to where we once were. I was in denial for so long, but I think I'm finally accepting the truth—I miss being close with her. And I don't mean just sex. I long to simply hold her again, maybe kiss her till she's breathless.

Of course, she's probably pissed as hell at me at the moment. I feel like crap, having to send back a text effectively dismissing her. Poor girl, all she wanted to do was go out and eat, just the four of us, like we did this afternoon.

It would've been fun too, if only Benny and Eliza weren't so into each other.

"You ready to go?" Benny asks once we're both fully dressed. "The other guys are already outside."

"Yeah," I sigh. "Guess I'm as ready as I'll ever be."

He cocks his head. "You sure you're up for this, dude? We could always do something else."

I feel bad that I didn't share with him that the girls wanted us to go to dinner. I don't know which he would've opted for if given a choice. But based on him being up for ditching the guys so readily, I think he'd have chosen the option where he could see Eliza again.

"Solvenson?" he prompts.

"Yeah, yeah, I'm good." I start heading for the locker room exit. "Let's get the fuck out of here."

At the gentlemen's club, it's the usual scene of drunken guys watching hot girls take off their clothes. And this is a club where *all* the clothes go.

The teammates we're out with are a couple of the newer young guys. They were called up from our minors system, so it's no surprise they're eager to impress me and Benny. They tip the doorman a bundle to secure us front row seats, and then they insist on buying the first round of drinks.

Before we can stop them, they're gone. But when they return with vodka tonics for everyone, one of them has to return to the bar to exchange one drink for soda water for Benny.

"I tried to tell you guys I don't drink anymore," he says to the player remaining.

"It's cool, man. Sobriety is something to be proud of."

"It is," I agree, giving Benny an *I'm proud of you* nod.

I am proud of him too. There was once a time he would've declined coming out. He spent several months post-rehab pretty much avoiding any and all social events where alcohol might be involved, which included most all outings last season. But after we won the Stanley Cup he started going out again. And since that day, he's been fine with hanging with us.

With that in mind, I turn to him and say, "It's great you can come out with us like this again."

"Yeah, it's just like old times, eh? But without the total craziness." He holds up his soda water, and I tap my glass to his. And then our attention is directed to the stage, where the first dancer is coming out.

"Shit, talk about a total girl-next-door look," I mutter as I tip my rocks glass back and take a drink.

It's true—this first girl looks like she just stepped off a college campus. I'm used to professionals—chicks with huge fake tits, big hair, and surgeon-sculpted bodies.

"You're right," Benny says. "She definitely does *not* look like your run-of-the-mill stripper."

One of the young guys leans in and informs us, "It's amateur night, so these are all fresh rookies."

"Cool." Benny nods approvingly. "Real girls taking off their clothes always beat the pros."

I can't disagree. And because I am a man before anything else, I proceed to sit back and enjoy the show.

RACK CITY, BITCH

LAINEY

"Uh, I don't know if we should do this," Eliza says as we approach the neon-bedecked gentlemen's club entrance. "I'm definitely having second thoughts."

"We'll be fine," I assure her.

She looks back longingly in the direction of the arena, but it's only a glimmer in the distance. We walked the couple of blocks down, having left our cars parked back at the Desert Sports Complex.

"We're here now." I point to the warehouse building with a medieval façade. "Let's give this thing a try."

"Yeah, but I think getting in is going to be harder than we thought." She points over to a large sign that's carved into the fake stone. "I mean, check out that sign stating *no women allowed*. It's freaking etched in stone, Lainey! I don't think they're going to bend the rules for us."

"How archaic," I retort, suddenly struck by how sexist the stupid rule is.

I say as much, and Eliza retorts, "Um, I think this place kind of epitomizes and thrives on sexism."

To illustrate her point, she gestures to the several neon-outlined naked girl silhouettes that line the front of the building.

"Well, it's a good thing I'm dressed like an employee. It'll be our ticket in." I lock my arm with hers, and we start up a set of metal steps that lead to a thick steel door manned by a big beefy bouncer, one who's eyeing us warily.

I lean in and whisper to Eliza, "Okay, here's the plan. I'm going to tell that guy I work here and that you want to come in with me so you can apply for a job."

God, I hope Nolan and Benny are really here. Otherwise, this is about to turn into a totally embarrassing experience.

"I just hope that works," she whispers back as we continue up the steps.

"It will," I reply.

But before we reach the top of the steps the bouncer jerks his huge thumb to indicate the side of the building.

We stop in our tracks, and he yells down to us, "You're a little late, ladies, but if you still want in the entrance for you is around the back."

"The entrance for us?" I mutter, confused. "I thought this place was strictly for the boys."

Even though I don't think he heard me, he scowls down at me, like how dare I question him. "Was I stuttering?" he says.

Eek! "Um, no."

"Get yours asses moving, then! Go around to the back!"

"Yes, sir," Eliza squeaks out as we spin around and hightail it down the stairs.

"He doesn't look like the kind of guy you mess with," Eliza remarks as we race around the side of the building to this supposed ladies-only entrance in the back.

I agree, and walk faster. Despite the detour and the little scare, I'm bolstered by the fact we haven't been shooed away completely.

We're here, and we're doing this! We're going to get in and shock the shit out of the guys. And I'm going to make sure Nolan is behaving, damn it!

This seems too easy, though, which worries me a little, prompting me to say to Eliza, "It's weird we didn't have to talk him into letting us in."

She shrugs. "Guess he already figures we work here. I mean, why else would we want in?"

"Yeah, I guess…"

The truth is, something is bothering me. I just can't pin what it is just yet.

I'm about to suggest giving up and going back to our cars, but just then we turn the corner and run right into a heavyset hulk of a man. We jump back, and he narrows his squinty eyes at us, looking none too happy.

I get the immediate impression that this scary dude is in charge around here. Maybe it's due to the fact he looks uncannily like the main mobster dude in the show *The Sopranos*. What was that character's name? Tony, right? Well, this is Tony on steroids.

"Maybe we should leave," Eliza whispers.

"I'm in total agreement," I mumble back.

But before we can spin around and make a run for it, Tony, in a commanding voice, barks out, "Hurry up and get your asses inside the building, ladies. The show's over and the other girls have left, but"—he eyes us both hungrily—"I think we can make an exception and squeeze you in."

"Squeeze us in for what?" I ask, wary. Surely, he doesn't mean for one of us to *dance?*

Tony doesn't supply an answer to my inquiry. Instead, he just reaches around with his big bearlike arm and shoves us through the propped-open back door, like neither of us weighs an ounce.

We're thrust into a sweaty-smelling dark hall and, as he slams the door shut, leaving us alone, Eliza spits out, "Who the hell does he think he is?" She places her hand on the closed door, ready to go back out. "The bouncer at the front door was bad enough, but at least he didn't touch us. This guy, though… I have a few things to say to him."

When she starts to turn the handle, to go bitch out Tony—*is she nuts?*—I yank her away and pull her deeper into the dark corridor.

"What's gotten into you?" I hiss. "You were scared of the guy in the front. What makes you think you can take on Tony?"

"Who?"

"Tony Soprano, from the TV show about the mafia. That guy looks just like him. And you want to go argue with him. Do you have a death wish?"

She rolls her emerald eyes at me. "Oh, stop. He just made me mad, is all. And for the record, just because he looks like a mobster doesn't mean he is one, Lainey. I'm sure he just works here, like the guy in the front. You're so dramatic sometimes."

"Let's just not antagonize him. Please."

"Okay, fine." She sighs. "But what do we do now? This was your grand plan, remember? And now we're stuck in this dark, creepy hallway, nowhere near the guys."

"Hey, we're in, right? I say we make our way to the audience area. That's where we'll find the guys." I purse my lips, glancing left and right. "Let's just choose a direction and see where it leads."

Eliza finally settles down. "Okay, let's do this."

I smirk, back on plan myself. "This might work out better than coming in through the front. For the surprise factor, you know? The guys would *never* expect us to emerge from the back."

"If they're even here," she says, sounding suddenly worried they might not be and all this grief will be for nothing.

"Don't worry. I have a feeling they are." *Crap, I hope I'm right.*

And then, like it's meant to be, I swear I hear Nolan's low-timbre laugh. I listen more closely and detect the muffled murmuring of male voices from the left side of the hall.

"This direction must be the way to the audience," I say, pointing down that way. "Come on, let's hurry."

We start walking so quickly that we may as well just jog. And we do for about twenty seconds. Then we're brought to a screeching halt when a very tall, very busty blonde woman, one squeezed into a tight red sequined gown like a sausage, just about bowls us over.

"Oh, sorry," she says, stepping back and tottering on her high heels. Narrowing her heavily lined eyes at us, and tapping a pointy fingernail to her pink-glossed mouth, she adds, "Hmm, I thought we were done for the night. All the other girls have left. Did Gus let you in?"

Assuming that's Tony, I nod.

She sighs. "I can see why he sent you in, but it is awfully late."

Eliza and I look at each other and shrug.

She looks us over then, like real thoroughly. After a minute, she turns to continue down the hall, beckoning for us to follow.

We do, and I hear her muttering to herself, "What the hell. We still have a decent-sized crowd. It's just a shame I can only fit one of them in."

"What's she blabbering about?" Eliza whispers to me as we continue to follow the blonde. "Fit one of us in for *what* exactly?"

"I have no idea," I reply, though I have a sneaking suspicion, one I've suspected but denied to myself, since Tony/Gus shoved us into this place.

My suspicion is confirmed when we turn a corner and step into a brightly lit room. It's a dressing room, lined with tables, lighted mirrors, makeup, and hair products. There are several glittery costumes strewn about, as well.

"Shit." I turn to Eliza. "She must think we're here to dance."

Eliza's eyes widen and her face pales. "Dance, like where? Up on the stage?"

I draw in a stuttered breath. This is worse than I thought. "I think so."

Eliza hisses, "Now who's the crazy one? *I'm* not going out there and shaking my booty for a roomful of horny men."

Busty Blonde is watching our exchange, hands on her hips. In a chastising tone, she politely informs us, "Now is not the time to develop a case of the nerves."

With her gaze resting on me, likely because of my attire, she says, "I do have to tell you that I love this look you've come up with for tonight. It's kind of a like a hockey whore chic, yes?"

I glance over at Eliza. "Told you I looked like a puck bunny on the prowl!"

She shrugs, and Busty Blonde quickly says, "No, no, this look is perfect. We have a few Wolves players out in the audience tonight, and this'll play perfectly for a grand finale."

This confirms that the guys are here. Still, am I really going to go out and dance on a stage in front of a roomful of horny men? And what about the disrobing part? I could always just take off the jersey and corset and leave the rest.

Swallowing hard, I turn to Eliza. My expression pleads for her to tell me what to do.

"It's up to you, Lainey," she says.

"If I go out there, it may be worth the humiliation. Nolan likes strippers so much? Well, let's see how much he likes them when it's *me* up on the stage. It's sure to drive him nuts, way more than me just showing up here."

"It probably would," she agrees.

Now that I have clarity of purpose—teaching Nolan a lesson that two can play at the strip club game—I'm warming to the idea of dancing.

"How hard can it be?" I go on. "I've danced around my bedroom a million times, listening to music and sometimes even pretending to take off my clothes."

"There's no pretending here," Busty Blonde interjects.

Gulp.

"You're really going to do it?" Eliza asks.

"Yeah"—I nod—"I think I am."

Shaking her head, but looking at me like I'm her new hero, she says, "Wow. You're way braver than I am."

When I turn to inform Busty Blonde it's a go, I'm face-to-face with a huge can of hair spray she has in her hand.

"Bend at the waist," she instructs. "And flip back your hair."

I comply, and she sprays my resulting sex-bed hair into place. She lifts my Wolves jersey up an inch, and I protest, "Hey! My strip tease doesn't start back here, does it?"

"No, but I need to see what you have on underneath."

Sighing, I wave my hand. "Fine, lift away."

Once my black skirt is revealed, she nods approvingly. "That's cute. Nice and short. Are you wearing panties underneath?"

"Boy shorts."

"And up under here?" She taps my chest, right on Nolan's number.

I list off, "A black corset, a white blouse under that, and a bra. It's my waitressing uniform."

"Are you a cocktail waitress?"

"Yes."

"You should make much better tips here."

"Yeah, but I don't have to take off my clothes where I work," I mutter.

Sighing, she says, "Can I give you a few pointers for when you're out there?"

"Please."

"Skimpy as your clothes are, you have a few layers to work with, which is good. I'd suggest drawing out your act." She winks at me. "If you can make it last two songs, you'll receive a hell of a lot more cash."

I can't believe I'm really going through with this.

"When you're down to nothing," she goes on, "just go ahead and place any bills you receive in the glass jar at the back of the stage."

It finally catches up to me what I just heard.

"Wait, what? What do you mean when I get down to nothing?"

"We do full nude stripping here," she replies nonchalantly, like it's no big deal.

Eek, what? "Um, I might be reconsidering here."

"Sweetie, it's too late." She shoves me up a riser that leads to the stage. Behind the thick dark curtain, I hear "Rack City" by Tyga start to play. A man then announces that there's one more act, a surprise grand finale.

So much for backing out now.

I can do this. What's a little skin? Plus, maybe I won't even get that far. I'll probably be so bad I'll get booed off the stage.

I start to remove the hockey jersey, suddenly feeling weird about Nolan seeing it, but she yells up to me, "Leave it till you hit the stage. The hockey players out there are going to love it."

Maybe the others, I think, *but not Nolan.* Not when it's *his* jersey I'm wearing. And definitely not when he realizes it's *me* stripping. My backhanded attempt to give him a taste of his own medicine is turning out to be more than I anticipated.

I'm in it now, though, whether I want to be or not.

May as well embrace your inner stripper goddess and give these boys a show.

Glancing back at Eliza, I mouth, "Here goes nothing."

She gives me an encouraging thumbs-up and calls up to me, "You go, girl. Break a leg."

Knowing me, that might actually happen.

"No, you'll be fine," I whisper to myself.

I then take a deep breath…and step out onto the stage.

YOU GOTTA BE F*CKING KIDDING ME

NOLAN

The beat of Tyga's "Rack City" fills the room, but there seems to be a delay in getting the next girl out.

Funny, I thought the show was over. But then there was an announcement about a surprise grand finale.

"Probably a last-minute addition," Benny says.

"Yeah, probably," I agree.

When the delay continues, he goes on. "Must be a case of rookie nerves. You remember what it was like the first time you were about to hit the ice with the big boys. This is probably kind of the same."

I laugh. "Only you, Benny, would think to compare playing in the NHL for the first time to stripping."

The next girl finally comes out before he has a chance to reply.

Wow, there's a lot of fanfare with this one. All the flashing strobe lights and crisscrossing spotlights are so blinding that I can barely make out that there's a girl up on stage. But then I see her standing there, seemingly unsure what to do next. I also see she's wearing something red and black.

Wait! This next "amateur" has on my fucking sweater. "What the hell?"

"See, man," Benny says, nudging me. "Looks like you were wrong, great sensei. There *is* a correlation between hockey and stripping."

I chuckle, since this couldn't have played out more perfectly for him.

"Touché," I say.

I'm convinced the stripper wearing the hockey sweater with my number on it must be something the young guys put her up to. But then I'm not so sure, seeing as they're whooping and hollering like it's all a surprise to them too.

The girl tentatively steps forward and starts gyrating her slim hips. She's moving a little awkwardly, but it's still sexy as hell.

More hollering ensues.

Usually men are a little quieter, not at all like women when they watch guys strip. But I think this girl's hot outfit, and her even hotter body, have them more wound up than usual.

The lights glaring in my face are still too bright for me to get a good look at the dancer's face, but damn if there isn't something familiar about her body.

...And those thigh-high boots.

...And that long hair she's swinging around like a metal band guitarist. The dark, rich color reminds me of—

"What the fuck? That's Lainey up there!"

Benny pulls back the twenty-dollar bill he was trying to lure her over with, like it just burned his hand.

"Shit, Nolan." He stuffs the money back in his pocket, his expression sheepish. "I had no idea. But now that I look a little closer"—he squints into the glare—"I think you might be right."

"I know it's her," I grind out. "I don't need confirmation. What the hell is she doing here? And more importantly, why in the hell is she up on the fucking stage?"

Benny shrugs, and I'm at a loss. I'm also ready to risk the wrath of the roaming bouncers and security guards by hauling my own ass up on the stage so I can drag her off, especially when the younger guys, who have no idea who the girl is, keep right on whooping it up.

"Take off the jersey!" one of them yells.

"Fuck that," the other chimes in. "Take it all off, baby."

I glare over at my oblivious teammates.

"What's up your ass, Solvenson?" the one who wants her to *take it all off* asks. "You should be pulling out money to get her over here. It's *your* fucking number she has on."

"Yes, she does, doesn't she?" I reply tightly.

Meanwhile, Lainey is up there swishing around the hem of the sweater, the one with *my* number on it, making it ride up just enough to reveal the short skirt underneath.

Oh, I know that skirt well. It's part of her waitressing uniform, which means she has on a few layers, skimpy though they are, to drag this thing out.

Good, that gives me time to figure out how to get her out of this mess.

But until then, I have to suffer. And help me Lord, suffer I do. It's pure misery watching the men go crazy when Lainey starts peeling off the sweater to reveal her whole sexy bar wench ensemble.

I know the feeling, boys, that fucking outfit makes me hard every time I see her in it.

I would be in an aroused state now, except I have other things weighing on my mind. Things like killing the strange guy I just noticed at the far end of the stage. He's beckoning Lainey over so he can slide a fiver in the waistband of her skirt.

And she lets him!

When she proceeds to smile and toss her sweater into the crowd, I stand up. *That's enough.*

Benny grabs my arm. "What do you think you're doing, Solvenson. You'll get thrown out of here before you make it two feet up on that stage."

He's right, so I sit back down. "For now, I'll stay put," I snap. "But if she starts taking any part of that uniform off, besides the corset, I'm getting up there and dragging her ass to the back, repercussions be damned."

"The other amateurs took everything off," Benny reminds me. "There's no reason why she won't too."

I glare at him. "She's not a wannabe stripper, Benny. I don't know why she's here, but I can assure you it's not to try out for a job."

That was the lure of this amateur night, or so we were told shortly before the performances started. We were highly encouraged to make the most noise for the dancers we liked best. Based on the amount of cheers and catcalls Lainey's receiving at the moment, I have no doubt this place would hire her in a minute.

Over my dead body.

Lainey eventually works her way over to our side of the stage, and I finally can see her whole face. Hmm, doesn't she look smug, even going so far as to blow me a *take that, Nolan* kiss.

Our eyes meet, and there's a ton of unspoken communication.

What the fuck do you think you're doing up there? I try to say with my questioning glare.

I imagine her retorting, *showing you I can do whatever I want. You like strippers so much? Well, I like being one. Watch me dance, Nolan.*

And dance she does.

Lainey grabs the pole at the center of the stage, wraps one leg around it and throws her head back as she spins her way down. The whole audience is given a flash of the boy shorts she wears under her skirt. She learned the first night on the job that panties don't offer much coverage, as proven when I tore them off her during our little tryst.

Nonetheless, boy shorts are enough to wind the men up even more. Chants of "take it off, take it all off" echo off the walls, louder than the music even, which has moved on to a second song, an oldie but goodie and strip show staple, "Pour Some Sugar on Me" by Def Leppard.

Lainey glances around, and I can tell she's unsure of what to do next. She bites her lower lip and glances over at me. She knows I'll rescue her if she wants. But just so there's no doubt, I give her a reassuring nod.

One of the bouncers, a huge man with a bald head, sees me communicating with her and rightly suspects I'm up to something. He heads over to where the boys and I are seated.

"No funny stuff," he mutters down to me as he crosses his big beefy arms and glares.

He's not glaring at me for long, though. No, the prick turns his gaze to Lainey up on the stage, a hungry gleam in his dark eyes.

That infuriates me even further.

Lainey, eyes still on me, pleading by this point, shakily undoes her corset and tosses it out to the crowd. She then starts to lift her flouncy bar wench top up over her head, and then it's off. She closes her eyes tightly, like she's wishing she could disappear, and flings the shirt out into the crowd, leaving her breasts, though thankfully covered by a bra, on full display.

The crowd goes nuts.

She does have awesome tits, definitely the best of the night. And though we're just friends—I'm beginning to despise those words, by the way—I can't help but feel a strong sting of possessiveness.

"That's enough gawking at my girl," I mutter, making Benny look over at me curiously.

"Thought you two were just friends," he says.

I give him a look, and he knows then that we're *not* "just friends."

That's why he doesn't stop me when I jump up on the stage.

And that's why he holds back the bald bouncer as long as he can, giving me more than enough time to reach Lainey and cover her up with my suit jacket.

But no sooner is that taken care of that I hear someone—her—yell, "Nolan, look out!"

The next thing I know, I'm tackled to the ground by three burly men.

18

MY KNIGHT IN SHINING ARMOR

LAINEY

I try to warn Nolan, but three bouncers swoop in from three different angles and tackle him to the ground.

"Stop it," I scream as I tug on one's long hair. "Leave him alone."

"We're doing this for *your* protection," a bald one barks.

"You don't need to protect me," I protest. "He's not a threat. I know him, okay? I freaking know him."

I can't tell if they're listening to me, or just moving forward with their protocol in dealing with an unruly patron, but the next thing I know they're hoisting Nolan up, and then dragging him off to the little dressing room with the costumes and the makeup and the mirrors.

I follow, leaving the stage. Nobody stops me, but the men in the audience start booing. I guess they're pissed I left without finishing the show. Too bad. My stripping days are officially over.

In the dressing room, things calm down. I still rush over to see if Nolan is all right, but I end up backing off. The bald bouncer takes Nolan aside, I guess to speak with him, and I figure I shouldn't interrupt lest things re-escalate.

The other two bouncers give me no more than a passing glance before they walk over to the other side of the room to join their bald compatriot, and Nolan. I'm left standing in the center of the room, so I scan around for Eliza, or even the busty blonde lady, but neither one is here.

One of the bouncers comes back over, the one whose hair I was pulling, and I ask, "Where's my friend?"

"Who do you mean? The redhead?" I nod, and he informs me, "Oh, her. We sent her away."

"Why'd you do that?"

"No women are allowed in this club unless they're dancing." His eyes move to my chest, which is semi-exposed, despite the fact I have on a bra and Nolan's suit jacket is still draped over my shoulders.

I slip my arms into the big sleeves and pull the jacket tightly around me, mumbling, "Perv."

The bouncer dude chuckles, amused. He then jerks his thumb over to where Nolan is still speaking with the other two bouncers. Hell, even though Nolan's tie is askew and his white dress shirt has a tear in the arm, he's laughing and joking with the men who just tackled him.

And wait, what's that going on now? Is that a Wolves ballcap he's signing for the big, bald one?

"Men." I shake my head and say to Long Hair, "It's amazing how you guys can be ready to rip each other's throats out one minute, and then be all best buddies the next."

Long Hair lets out a laugh. "It doesn't always end up like this. Your buddy over there is lucky he's a star in this town. Otherwise, we'd have thrown him out on his ass. But not before getting in a few good shots."

"Ha," I snort, "you could've tried. You clearly haven't seen Nolan on the ice when he gets into a fight. It doesn't happen often, but when it does he never loses."

It's true—Nolan kicks ass in all ways on the ice. He even got a Gordie Howe hat trick one game last season when he scored a goal, an assist, and got into a fight.

"Yeah, but there's only one of him," the bouncer retorts, puffing up. "And there're three of us."

"I guess you have a point," I concede.

Long Hair leaves me to return to where Nolan is wrapping up with the other guys. He must want something autographed too. Everyone ends up shaking hands and clapping each other on the back, as men are wont to do. When they finally disperse, Nolan joins me.

I plop down on a metal folding chair, because, well, I am exhausted.

"You look tired," Nolan remarks, pulling up another metal chair so he can sit across from me.

"I am," I reply, yawning. "Exotic dancing is way more grueling than I thought it'd be."

"Speaking of which…" He raises a brow and nods to my half-clothed body. "What exactly *are* you doing in this place?"

"Crashing your little night out," I reply, smug. But when he starts shaking his head, clearly disappointed, I admit, "Okay, okay, maybe crashing a 'gentlemen's club'"—I make little air quotes and roll my eyes dramatically—"wasn't such a great idea."

"You think?"

"Smartass," I murmur. "But in my defense," I go on, "I had no freaking idea it was amateur night."

"Yeah, well, what I don't get is why you came here in the first place. You texted you were going out to eat with Eliza. What the hell went wrong?"

"That actually was the plan…at first." I sigh. "But when you sent back the text nixing that idea, it got us wondering what you were up to. We couldn't imagine where you and Benny could be going that we couldn't come along."

Nolan shakes his head, muttering, "Women. You just can't leave well-enough alone, can you?"

"We are persistent," I admit.

"That's for sure," he agrees. And then he asks, "How'd you figure out where we were going?"

"Eliza heard her dad bitching about this place the other day. She had a feeling you guys might be coming here. It was the most logical explanation as to why we couldn't come along."

He looks around. "Where is Eliza, anyway?"

"That annoying bouncer with the long hair said he sent her away. Apparently, they're pretty strict in enforcing that no-women-allowed rule. Unless you're dancing, of course."

Nolan shoots me an annoyed look, not needing a reminder, I'm sure.

Ignoring him, I continue. "I guess Eliza walked back to the arena to get her car. Which reminds me"—I reach for my purse that I left on the floor before I hit the stage and take out my phone—"I should text her and make sure she's all right."

As I start typing a message, Nolan clears his throat, loudly. I glance up to find him looking more displeased with me than he was three minutes ago.

"What now?" I ask as I finish my text and hit *Send*.

"You walked down from the arena dressed in your work uniform?" he says tightly.

Nolan loves and hates my cocktail waitress outfit. He loves that it's skimpy and sexy and works him all up, but he hates that other men get to see me in it.

Eliza texts back that she's fine. Then she asks how I'm doing and if I survived my first stripper-ing experience.

I text back, *I'm good. I lucked out and didn't have to take off all my clothes.*

No way. How'd you manage that?

Nolan rescued me, I inform her.

Wow. You'll have to fill me in on all the details later.

I will.

"Lainey, I asked you a question," Mr. Impatient cuts in.

I put my phone away and snap, "I had a jersey on over everything, okay? The one I threw into the crowd."

"Yeah, I don't remember you having that."

"I bought it before the game."

"You did?"

"Yes, Nolan, I did."

He smiles, his expression softening. "I noticed it had my number on it."

I smile back. "Of course I'd choose your jersey. Do you really think I'd wear one of your teammates' numbers?"

"I'd hope not."

"Well, I wouldn't," I assure him.

He releases a breath. "Lainey, I—"

"Wait," I interrupt as I realize my brand-new jersey is probably gone, along with all my other discarded clothing. "Crap," I mutter.

"What's wrong?" he asks.

I gesture at my chest, covered only by my bra since his suit jacket is gaping open. It doesn't matter; Nolan's seen it all many times.

"I threw my new jersey out in the crowd. My corset and waitress blouse are gone too." I sigh. "The casino's going to be so pissed at me. I'm sure I'll have to pay to replace the stuff."

"Hmm, maybe not." Nolan glances over to where he and the bouncers were talking earlier.

Standing, he holds up a finger and says, "Hold on a sec, I'll be right back."

He walks over to a nearby table, and when he returns, I take note of what he's carrying.

Happy, I blurt out, "Yay, my clothes!"

He hands me the small pile of clothing. "One of the bouncers mentioned that Benny and the boys rescued your stuff from the masses. They made him and my other teammates leave, but not before they got your clothes back from them."

"Thank you," I say.

Nolan makes a face. "Still, I wouldn't put any of it on till you've washed everything. Who knows what kind of derelicts handled that stuff."

I peer down at the blouse, corset, and jersey. When I lift the items up to my nose and take a tentative whiff, I can't help but make a face. "Yuk. It all smells like beer."

"Like I said, just wash everything."

Softly, I say, "Hey, look, I'm sorry for putting you in a position where you had to save me. Thank you for doing so, though."

I glance over at him, expecting more consternation. But instead of looking aggravated or annoyed, he's smiling over at me. That's the thing about Nolan I adore—he can be mad as hell over something, but forgive just as quickly.

"I'll always come to your rescue, Lainey," he tells me.

"Just like at the movie when I was scared?"

"Just like."

"So you're my knight in shining armor, eh?"

"Eh?"

"What can I say, Nolan? I'm picking up your Canadianisms. You should have seen me earlier. I was even calling my jersey a sweater."

Chuckling, he insists, "It *is* a sweater, Lainey."

"If you say so."

"I do."

We laugh, and he stands and reaches for my hand. I take it, and he lifts me to my feet.

Facing each other, our bodies mere inches apart, I straighten his crooked tie and tell him again, "I really am sorry you had to get into a fight over me."

"It's okay." He tucks a strand of wayward hair behind my ear. "But you never answered my question about *why* you were even here. Did you come just to make me jealous? If so, I can assure you, it worked."

I come clean, since he deserves the truth. "It was meant as a joke. At least, that's how I sold the idea to Eliza, insisting it'd be funny as hell if we actually got in and crashed your little men-only outing. But like I said before, I had no idea it was damn amateur night."

He cocks his head, peering down at me. "You said 'sold the idea to Eliza.' What was your real reason, Lainey?"

I look up into his crystal-blue eyes and bite my lip. "I wanted to make sure you didn't do anything stupid, Nolan."

He shakes his head, blows out a breath, and says, "Jesus, Lainey.

You're never going to let me live down that Marty Quick interview, are you?"

"Would you do it again? Sleep with a bunch of strippers?"

I feel like I have to know, and waiting for him to reply is tortuous.

But, at last, he says softly, "No, I wouldn't."

There's something in his voice, something different from the Nolan he's shown me so many times, leading me to ask, "Why not?"

He cradles my face, his warm palm lingering on my cheek. "I think those crazy days are behind me, Lainey."

I want more. I want to know if this change of heart is because of me. But we're supposed to be "just friends," and friends don't ask each other these kinds of questions.

But I have to know, so my eyes search his. Is he looking for a go-ahead from me so we can drop this farce and move forward? I'm ready to, but I need something from him first.

"Nolan, how do you feel about me?" I tap his chest. "Like in here, deep in your heart, in your soul even. Do you feel me in there? Are we more than just friends? And I don't mean just the sex part. I know we'll always have that kind of crazy draw to one another. What I'm asking is if you feel *more*?"

He drops his hand, and I feel his walls going up.

"What do you mean exactly?" he says, hedging already. "You know I care deeply for you, Lainey. Didn't I just demonstrate as much? Actions speak louder than words, don't you think?"

"Sometimes a woman needs *the words*, Nolan."

He blows out a breath. "Lainey, I—I, uh..."

Say the words, Nolan, just freaking say the goddamn words. Tell me you love me. Because it may have taken me this long to realize it, but I finally know I definitely love you.

I think all this, but really I'm just as bad as him. I can't bring myself to pour out my heart anymore than he can.

I look up at him, and he stares down at me. Is he waiting for the same, for me to say the words first?

I open my mouth.

He eyes me expectantly, one brow going up.

But in the end, I can't do it.

I *need* him to go first. He dumped me back in the spring, and he kept his secret from me for months. Hell, he fucked strippers, for heaven's sake! I just can't be the one who capitulates, not this time. I came up with this friends-thing for this exact reason. And it's not going to end till he cares enough about me to take a chance and put his heart out there.

"Say it first, Nolan," I whisper encouragingly, giving him a chance.

Shaking his head, he holds out his hand and simply says, "Let's get you home, Lainey."

19

SO MUCH FOR FOLLOW-THROUGH, SOLVENSON

NOLAN

I know what Lainey wants, but I'm not there just yet.

Will I ever be?

I don't know.

I'd like to think so, but all I know at the moment is my perfectly structured world is upside down. I need to talk to someone. I'd like to ask the person who's become my best friend, Lainey, for advice. But she's the reason for all the confusion in the first place.

I turn instead to the one guy I know can help, at least on this topic—Brent.

"Hey, man." I catch up with him before he leaves the ice at the end of an early morning practice. "You okay with hanging back a sec? There's something I want to ask you about."

Turning to me and leaning on his stick, he says, "Sure, man. What's up?"

After making sure everyone is off the ice and on their way back to the locker room, and therefore well out of earshot, I blow out a breath. "Hey, skate with me for a minute. I can't stay still right now. I need to be moving to think straight."

Brent eyes me curiously. "Sure, but this isn't like you, Solvenson."

We start skating, and I murmur, "Tell me about it."

At first, we say nothing at all. I come upon a stray puck left behind from practice and wrist it into a nearby net.

Finally, I look over and say to Brent, "It's about Aubrey's sister."

"Ah, Lainey…"

He doesn't look remotely surprised, so I flat out ask, "You've known all along that's there's been something going on between us, haven't you?"

"I have," he confirms. "Not for sure definite, but I started suspecting after your New Year's Eve party."

"What tipped you off?" I laugh. "All the flirting she and I did that night?"

Chuckling, he says, "Nah. I caught her coming in the next morning."

"Ah, now it all makes sense. I bet she was looking well and freshly fucked, eh?"

"You're such a smug fucker." He laughs. "But you could say that, yeah."

We're kidding around, but I'm serious when I ask, "Does Aubrey know?"

He shakes his head. "No. I've never mentioned a word to her about that morning. I figure if Lainey wants to tell her, she will."

I nod, agreeing. "That's always been my thinking on the subject too."

"So where do you two stand right now?" His tone suddenly brims with doubt as he says, "Are you *really* just friends these days?"

"Believe it or not, Brent, and despite what's happened in the past, we really are trying the just-friends route, for now."

"Wow, so it's not all an act?"

"Nope."

I guess my frustration on the subject is showing, since Brent next says, "And how's that working out for you?"

"Not good," I admit. "Not good at all."

I come across another stray puck, wind my stick up, and slam the vulcanized rubber disk hard as I can down the ice. Brent lets out a low whistle when the puck smacks off the boards and ricochets back to where we're stopped.

"Clearly," he replies.

I let out a snort. We start skating again, in silence, until Brent quietly asks, "Does Lainey know what went down in your past?"

"I assume you're referring to my miserable foray into marriage. And yeah, I told her everything."

"Did it spook her? Is that why you two went the friends-route?"

"No, I'm afraid we were already well on our way down *that* miserable path when I came clean."

"Guess that ensured you stayed on it, eh?"

"You could say that."

Brent glances over at me knowingly. "And now you two are stuck and don't know how to move forward."

I laugh. "I knew coming to you was the right move."

"Watch out, Solvenson," he says, teasing. "I might end up taking over your role as team sensei."

I bark out a laugh. "What, captain not good enough for you?"

He shoots me the bird, and tells me to "fuck off."

This is why we're friends. There's no bullshit when we talk. We straight-up tell it like it is. And that's what Brent's does when he then says, "You want my advice?

"That's why I'm talking to you."

"Make a move, my friend. One of you has to. But make sure it's a bold move. If you want Lainey let her know with the kind of action that leaves no doubt."

I think about me saving her at the strip joint, and how that wasn't enough. Not without the words I couldn't say afterward.

"What about post-bold move, Brent? What would you do then?"

He shrugs. "Hard to say, but if Lainey's anything like Aubrey, you better be ready to talk."

"You're not kidding." I chuckle, and add, "You really do know these Shelburne women, don't you?"

"I guess I do. Aubrey, for sure, but Lainey seems the same. They're pretty much like all women, man. They want to hear the fucking words."

Shit, I'm unsure what Lainey needs me to say, like specifically. I can't ask Brent for help with that. Only I can figure that one out. Besides, he's helped me enough today.

"Hey, thanks for listening to me," I say. "And thank you for definitely offering some sound advice."

"Anytime," he replies. "And Nolan?"

"Yeah?"

"Good luck."

With Brent's words of encouragement urging me on, I drive home from the rink with a budding plan. At my house, I change into swim trunks and head down to my pool. I pick up my phone once I'm there and invite Lainey over for a swim.

Today is the day. I need to make that move, so I'm happy when she accepts.

After she arrives, there's some friendly banter between us, and definitely lots of flirting, especially once we're situated on chaise lounges by the pool and lying under the scorching desert sun.

But then things falter a little when Lainey starts trying to convince me—unsuccessfully, I might add—that we "must" arrange a nondate double date with Eliza and Benny.

"It's a fabulous idea," she says as she spritzes water all over her smooth, shapely legs.

I adjust my sunglasses so she can't see I'm looking at her sexy body, and reply, "Uh, yeah, no. I don't think so."

Hot body, hot sun, steaming hot thoughts—hell, I'm ready to jump in the pool to cool my ass down. Out of those three options, the only safe one to focus on is the sun. So I do that, thinking about how I can't believe we're this far into October and it's still hot as a motherfucker.

Shit, times like these I miss Toronto like crazy. This time of the year we should be feeling the cool bite of autumn in the air, along with the accompanying icy promise that winter is coming. Don't even get me started on the leaves. There's no changing foliage around here. Not that there are all that many trees in the first place. It's more like cacti-land central.

Shit, I miss back east so much that I even miss the motherfucking snow. What I really miss, though, are the dynamics of change. Everything is stasis here—sunny every goddamn day. That's why I can't wait for our upcoming road games in western Canada. Once we're up in Vancouver, Calgary, and Winnipeg—the cities we'll be playing in—I can count on a good dose of how it *should* be this time of year.

"Are you even listening to me, Nolan?" I hear Lainey say.

"Yeah, I am," I lie.

Not only do I have no interest in setting up Benny and Eliza, but I'm having a hard time concentrating now that Lainey has turned on her side to talk to me. Her hot pink bikini was tempting enough when she was lying on the lounger normally, but now her full breasts are smooshed together and every curve, flat plain, and valley of her body is facing my way. It's impossible to think clearly when I want nothing more than to lean over and strip away those small pieces of fabric so I can lick her *every*where.

Now that would be a bold move, wouldn't it? For the time being, however, I need to pay attention to this nutty double-date nonsense. Otherwise, Lainey will start something that can't be stopped. Hell, I saw the way Benny and Eliza were eye-fucking each other at our lunch. They're one step away from actually fucking.

Yeah, that's not happening on my watch. I like Benny far too much to set him up in a no-win situation.

"No fucking way is that a good idea," I finally get around to articulating when Lainey reiterates how cute of a couple Benny and Eliza would make. "You do realize Coach T would probably run Benny over with a Zamboni if those two ever hooked up?"

Lainey rolls her eyes. "Highly unlikely, Nolan. God forbid he mess with his top line."

She has a point. Our top line, which consists of me at right wing, Brent at center, and Benny on the left, has been racking up points like nobody's business. It's ideally ideal. And Coach isn't about to screw with something that's working, leading me to concede, "Okay, he may not actually inflict bodily harm on Perry, but he could certainly make his life miserable. You wouldn't want that, now would you? Think of poor Benny."

Lainey looks torn. I know she likes Benny. Hell, everyone does. She wouldn't want him to suffer just because we—really just her—couldn't resist playing matchmaker.

Sure enough, and to my great relief, she finally gives in. "All right, Nolan. I guess I see your point." She sighs. "I'll nix the idea of the four of us going out next time Eliza brings it up."

"You should also discourage her from pursuing Benny on her own," I say.

She closes her eyes and scrunches up her face. "Ugh, I hate this. I'm all for seeing people get together, not for plotting ways to keep them apart."

Whoa, a loaded statement if I've ever heard one.

My reply is just as loaded. "I know, Lainey, but sometimes keeping people apart is for the best."

"You're such a cynic."

"And you know why."

We share a look filled with meaning. But quickly—way too quickly—both of us look away. I pick up her tube of sunscreen and pretend to read the back, like it's the most engrossing literature ever.

Lainey sighs. "Well, anyway, back to what we were talking about. Don't worry, I'll discourage Eliza. I'll make sure she knows the full extent of Benny's manwhoring ways."

"Be sure to tell her about his puck bunny directory."

Lainey gives me a look like I'm making this shit up. Too bad I'm not.

"Does he really have a PB directory?" Lainey inquires. "And if so, what's it like?"

"What do you think it's like? It's Benny's very own personal Yellow Pages for finding pussy."

"Nolan, that's disgusting."

"Sorry, but it's true."

I feel bad for encouraging this kind of shitty gossip about my friend, especially when he's actually cut down significantly on his once-steady stream of puck bunnies. But there are still a few, and there is a directory. Whoring around is the last addiction Benny's fighting.

Speaking of whoring around, Lainey really needs to lie back in the chair like a normal person. She's still twisted toward me, and now half a goddamn nipple is peeking out. I'm going to attack her if this persists. Though, come to think of it, maybe I should be doing that. It'd certainly be a bold move.

Pointing the tube of sunscreen at her luscious tits, and directly to the side with the nip slip, I say, "You want me to put some of this on your chest? You're looking a little pink right about there." I wiggle the tube and looking down, she finally notices how her bikini top has shifted and left a nip exposed.

"Nolan!" She hurries to cover up. "How long have I been like that?"

"Not long enough," I lament.

That earns me a scowl, and a reminder. "We're just friends, Nolan."

"What-the-fuck-ever."

Oh, now she's mad. "You...you..." Lainey picks up a towel and snaps it, hard as fuck, at my thigh.

"Ow, that shit hurts, you know," I bite out.

"Aww," she mocks, "poor little Nolan. Does he want me to kiss his tender skin and make it all better?"

So much for just-friends. I look over at her, raise a brow. "Is that an invitation?"

She's staring at my thigh area, where there is a developing red mark. But it's not her handiwork that holds her attention. No, she's focused on what's up a little higher—namely, my hard cock.

She lets out a little groan, all lusty-like, and that's all I need. I'm on her so fast she has no time to react.

Breathless, she presses back against the lounger. "Nolan, what are you doing?"

I tear my sunglasses off, and tossing them aside, I ask, "What does it look like I'm doing?"

With my arms caged around her, I watch her every move, evaluating her every reaction. She wants me, it's clear. But she's hesitating.

"Maybe we should discuss this first."

"Discussion later," I growl. "I have only one question for you right now."

"And that is…"

"Do you want me to touch you…love you…make you come?"

"Oh God, Nolan, you can't say things like that."

"Why the hell not? It's what I want to do."

"Yeah, but hearing you say those things makes me want that too."

"Good," I say softly, my hand in her hair, cradling her head. "That means we're on the same page."

When she doesn't resist, I reach down and part her legs. "Should I stop?" I ask as I lower my body to hers.

"No."

I center myself then, my full length pressed to her pussy. When I start dry-humping her slowly, she gasps, "Just this once, Nolan. And no fucking, okay?"

"Wait, what?"

I still, and she looks up at me and frowns. "Because we have to go back to being friends, Nolan, that's why. If I let you inside me, I won't be able to do that."

I think 'let you inside' might mean more than with my cock, but good. I'm done with this stupid friends farce. I'm ready to share my heart. I think. Though I'm not sure how much I should share. I'll worry about it later, after. My dick is too hard for me to think rationally right now.

I agree, albeit reluctantly, to her silly no-fucking stipulation. It's fine, as there are still many, many things I can do to her. Like slipping two fingers into her bikini bottoms, which I do now, and finding her slick and ready, start finger-fucking her.

"Lainey, fuck, you are so goddamn wet." I plunge into her again, stretching her. "I almost forgot how fucking tight you always are."

"So open me up, Nolan. I want you to make me yours."

"Oh, I'm going to," I assure her. And I am. I don't need my cock to do that.

Leaning down, I kiss her parted lips. But she's panting so much from me touching her that she has to turn away to catch her breath.

"The things you do to me…" she murmurs.

"Do you like?"

"Yes."

When she tightens around my fingers, I know she's close. Reaching down, she starts stroking my straining cock through my swim trunks. Soon, she's begging me to "take them off."

But taking them off would require moving, and Lainey's about to fall apart…

Ah, and then she does, bucking her hips, crying out my name.

After she comes back down to earth, she tells me, all sexy-like, "I want to suck you while you finger me some more."

"Fuck." I love when Lainey gets bossy *and* talks dirty.

I wrench down my swim trunks, complying with her request, and then move up to where her head is resting against the chair.

Carefully, I touch the tip of my cock to her soft lips, commanding her to, "Lick it, Lainey. Taste me."

She takes me into her mouth hungrily, like she can't get enough, and growling, I finally get her damn bikini bottoms off completely. I plunge three fingers in her, my thumb meanwhile working her clit.

Good "friend" that I am, and giving "friend" that she is, we spend the next half an hour using our fingers and mouths to make each other come over and over again, under the hot Vegas sun.

Only problem is afterward, no bold moves of the talking variety take place. There's no real discussion, not like I planned. There is a little bit of kissing, and a tender moment or two, but in the end neither of us says a word about what just happened. Nor do I share a thing about what's in my heart.

So much for follow through, Solvenson.

20

LIFE GOES ON

LAINEY

I thought he'd stop me from leaving. Maybe capture my wrist as I tied my bikini top back into place and beg me to stay so we could discuss what just happened.

But no, Nolan did nothing, even as I waited for him to do something.

Frustrated, I jumped up and glared down at him, aggravated beyond belief. He was back to lying on the chaise lounge and his eyes were closed like he had not a care in the world. I guess he'd gotten what he wanted.

Giving up on prolonging my anguish, I snapped, "I'm going home."

His eyes flew open, and since his sunglasses were lying over by the pool where he'd tossed them, he had to shield his gaze from the glaring sun with his hand.

"You don't have to leave," he said, squinting.

"Yeah," I replied, words clipped, "I actually really do."

I sensed hesitation on his part then. He looked like he was about to say something. And if there was ever a time he needed to speak, it was then. We'd just done something that deviated wildly from our carefully constructed friend-zone.

But had it all been doomed to fail from the start?

I think so. I can see that now.

I stared down at him. My one brow was raised the way he so often does. "Do you want to talk, Nolan? Like *really* talk?"

"Do you?" he threw back.

I sighed mightily. "I really think, at this point, I've said everything I could." *It's your turn now*, I thought, but didn't add. Maybe I should have, though, because he let me walk.

And here I am now, alone. That all happened yesterday, and I've still not heard a thing from him. There've been no texts, no calls. I could break and make the first move, but what would that prove? Only that I'm weak when it comes to Nolan, which I already so vividly displayed twenty-four hours ago when his dick was in my mouth.

Crap. I've already put too much on the line. It's bad enough he clammed up after saving me at the strip club. I should've known messing around with him would be a huge mistake.

And it is, was, shit. I need a break from him.

I guess that's why I'm feeling relieved he left to go on the road with the team early this morning. I know this because Brent's gone too. The Wolves are headed up to Canada for a long road trip, which should give me some much-needed time to think.

One thing for sure—this friendship biz has failed. I mean, come on. Bringing each other to orgasm out by the pool is not what friends normally do. Maybe they offer a shoulder to cry on, or hit up stores together. Grabbing lunch on your days off is good too. But the last time I checked, putting your friend's cock in your mouth—while said friend has his fingers buried so deeply inside you it feels like he's a part of you—is generally not typical buddy behavior.

Oh, who are you kidding? I stare at my reflection in the mirror above the dresser in my room. *You knew this was going to happen sooner or later. And really, look at you now. You may as well be wearing a freaking scarlet letter, declaring to the world what you did.*

Sighing, I turn my face from side to side, assessing the streaky sunburn I'm sporting, courtesy of yesterday's indiscretion. It's not gone unnoticed by Aubrey, either. She's been giving me curious glances ever since this morning. I was more discreet yesterday, but I made the mistake of emerging from my bedroom for breakfast makeup-less.

The problem is not just my sunburned—and now starting to peel—nose. It's that half my face is burned, and the other half is merely slightly tanned. It looks really funky. And for all you newbies out there, let this be a lesson learned—don't blow a guy with your head turned when under a scorching desert sun, especially not when your sunscreen has worn off.

I tried to reapply a fresh coat after our, uh, activities, but Nolan distracted me before I got to my face. In an uncharacteristic moment of unguarded tenderness, he pushed our chaise lounges so close together that when I turned to see what was up, our lips were inches apart.

He closed the gap before I could protest—not that I would have—and kissed the crap out of me.

It was sweet and tender, and I was so damn sure it'd lead to declarations of…something. Maybe love?

"Lainey," he murmured reverently against my lips when we came up for air.

I was breathless, dizzy, drunk on too many orgasms and now Nolan's lips. When I couldn't reply, he chuckled, and then he kissed me again.

I fell for him a little more in that moment. Okay, more like a *lot* more. That's why I was hoping we'd talk—like, *really* talk—after those unguarded moments of afterplay.

But, of course, that didn't happen.

The kissing ended, and we both grew quiet. He got up and moved our chairs apart. I swear he seemed like he was building up to say something. But he never did, and that's when I left.

I shake my head, watching me say *no* to my reflection in the mirror. "This can't go on," I say to my sad self.

Maybe it's time to do more than simply take a break from Nolan? We could always cut ties altogether, seeing as friendship isn't working. I just can't help but want more from him, more than he's willing to give.

Swallowing hard, because this option is far from appealing, I pick up a tube of concealer and start dabbing some onto my pink nose and left cheek. The burn was far more prominent yesterday, so when I arrived home from Nolan's, I locked myself in my bedroom and slathered on aloe vera gel and far more correcting makeup than I'm applying right now.

I had to do that before I faced anyone in the house.

My makeup was spot-on once I was done and no one suspected a thing for the rest of the day, not even Aubrey or Brent when we all ate dinner together. But then damn Brent had to stop by my room last night, *after* I'd washed off all the makeup. There was no time to run and reapply, so I thought "what the hell" and opened the door, greeting him with a Rudolph-red nose and half-red face.

He peered at me, perplexed as all get out. He opened his mouth to say something, but I held up my hand and swished it around, as if to say *stop right there.*

And then I actually did say, "Please, Brent, don't ask any questions or make a single smartass comment."

He nodded distractedly, still focused on my crazy burn.

"Okay," he said at last, "I won't say a word." He shook his head, looked away. "That's not why I stopped by, anyway."

I leaned my shoulder against the open door. "What's up? Is everything good with you and Aubrey?"

Brent sometimes comes to me to ask for little tips on how to deal with my sister, especially if she's PMS-ing. But from the utter adoration in his whiskey-colored eyes at the mere mention of Aubrey, I surmised there was no raging hormone issue.

Sure enough, softly and wistfully, the way only a man in love can do, he replied, "No, no, things are amazing with us."

"That's good." I smiled, truly happy for my sister and her beloved.

Brent hesitated then, running a cursory glance over my sunburn again. Finally, he blew out a long breath.

Uh-oh, is he gearing up to ask about me and Nolan?

Worried he might, I hurried him along, hoping he'd get to his point if I made a production of yawning.

"Oh my goodness," I said, covering my mouth. "I'm so sorry, Brent. I am just *so* exhausted. I guess being out in the sun half the day has made me extra sleepy."

I winced, realizing I'd brought his attention back to my funky sunburn. He knew I'd spent the afternoon at Nolan's. He had to be curious how I ended up with a half-burned face.

But Brent, taking the hint, finally got to the real reason for his visit. "Hey, I'm not here to keep you up. I just wanted to let you know you should expect a call from the Wolves' marketing department early tomorrow morning. The lady that runs the show over there could want you to be ready to interview as early as the afternoon."

"Wait, what?"

It was amazing news. A little short on notice, yes, but amazing nonetheless. *My days as a cocktail waitress might be mercifully numbered.* The job was easy early on, but ever since tourist and convention season went into full swing I've had to deal with handsy drunken patrons almost every night.

And it totally sucks.

Brent continued, "I heard from the head of marketing a short while ago. There's an opening, Lainey. She's talked with a bunch of applicants, but no one has stood out for her. Anyway, she has an open interview slot tomorrow afternoon. I don't know what time exactly, but she can tell you when she calls. I know it's not much notice. That's why I wanted to stop by and give you a head's u—"

I couldn't hold back any longer. I was too excited that I had a possible escape from cocktail waitress hell. I flung my arms around my future brother-in-law and squeezed him.

"Thank you so much, Brent." I bounced up and down on my toes as I stepped back. "I don't care if it's short notice. I already know a ton of stuff about the Wolves, from you and Aubrey and..." I stopped, not wanting to utter Nolan's name.

"It's only an entry-level position," he warned, having not even noticed my trailing off. "So you may want to table those hugs till you see if it's something you'd even be interested in."

"Are you kidding?" I snorted. "I don't care if it's nothing more than running around the city fetching coffee and doughnuts for the entire marketing team. Anything has to be better than getting pawed at every freaking night." *Oops, I said too much.*

His expression grew grim. "Is that what's happening down at the casino, Lainey?"

"Yes," I uttered in a small voice, not wanting to worry him. "But only a little bit."

He looked concerned. "Hey, if things ever get too out of hand, you let me know immediately. I'll be down there so fast people's heads will spin."

"Wow, thanks."

"It wouldn't be just me, either," he went on. "Nolan and Benny, and hell, even Dylan, we'd all have your back."

I felt warm and happy hearing that. I love these guys. One more than the others, of course, and in a much deeper way, but I truly care for all of them.

Smiling, I assured Brent, "It's nothing I can't handle. Even when it is we have security guards and bouncers on the premises to take care of things."

"Still, just remember we're here if you need us."

I replied a heartfelt, "Thanks, Brent."

He seemed to mull something over, before he then said, "You probably shouldn't mention any of this to Nolan. Let me talk to him first, especially if you ever really do need us. He'd go ballistic if he knew shit like that happens at your workplace."

Damn. Just as I suspected, Brent knows more than he lets on.

But he is right about one thing—Nolan. If he ever got wind of half the harassment I put up with from some of the customers, he'd blow a gasket. He'd sure as shit show up at the casino to defend me too. That'd land him in some hot water with the team. And me, I'd probably get fired on the spot. It'd just be a bad scene all the way around.

"I won't mention a word to him," I assured Brent. "I wasn't planning to, anyway."

He gave me a kind smile, and I saw what Aubrey sees in him. He's not only hot as hell, but he has a really sweet side. Who knew?

"Maybe it won't be a factor much longer," he said. "If you get this marketing job you could quit the casino."

"And I would," I replied.

Brent gave me the details of who would be calling, some lady named Mrs. Fielding, and I thanked him again.

So here I am now, preparing for the actual interview. Mrs. Fielding did indeed call this morning, and my slot is for three this afternoon.

It's now two o'clock.

Crap, I can't be late!

I finish my makeup and dress in my best navy blue interview skirt, low heels, and blouse, all in record time. I'm actually early when I arrive at the Desert Sports Complex. I'm ready for this interview, armed with numerous notes from the research I stayed up late gathering on the team's latest marketing efforts. I know a lot about the team itself, but I didn't know much about their current strategies. I do now. Still, as I walk into the building, despite all my preparation, nerves overtake me. This is my first big interview since graduating, and I can't blow it.

Mrs. Fielding, a nice, unassuming middle-aged lady, welcomes me into her office. We shake hands, and she motions for me to take a seat across from her desk.

"Please, make yourself comfortable, Ms. Shelburne." she says.

I thank her as I sit down and cross my legs, carefully so my skirt doesn't ride up.

Mrs. Fielding stops at a little cart littered with bottled waters, a full coffeepot, and Styrofoam cups. "Would you like anything to drink?" she asks. "The selections are limited, but I do have coffee and water."

I see she's pouring coffee for herself, so I ask for the same. "Coffee would be wonderful, thank you."

May as well follow the piece of interview advice I came across last night, encouraging interviewees to ingratiate themselves with representatives of the company by showing just how alike you are, and thus how perfectly you'd fit in.

Look, I'm part of the team already! I try to convey as I accept the coffee from Mrs. Fielding. I take a sip exactly when she does. But then she looks at me strangely, especially when I set my cup down on the desk at the exact same second she does. I reconsider this strategy, thinking, *hmm, maybe I'm laying it on a little too thickly.*

I quickly pick up my coffee and take a big gulp. But yikes, it's piping hot and I almost spit it out.

"You seem nervous," Mrs. Fielding says, while I grimace, swallowing the burn in my throat.

"I am a little," I admit once my mouth is no longer on fire.

"There's no reason to feel uneasy, Ms. Shelburne. You come very highly recommended." She pauses, and then adds, "By three parties, in fact. That's why someone as young as yourself, and with no experience, is here for this interview. The position may be listed as entry-level, but we tend to fill even those with highly-qualified individuals."

Gulp, I don't know if that's me.

But three parties have recommended me. Three. Interesting. I know Mrs. Fielding is not at liberty to divulge who any of them are, but that's okay. I'm already aware Brent and Aubrey put in a good word for me. But did Nolan vouch for me, as well? Maybe he wants me to stick around for the long term. But what would that mean? Probably just that he wants more of the same. And that makes me sad.

I'm elated if he did indeed put a good word in for me, but we still need to end it. It still doesn't make it any less depressing that he's not ready for a relationship, and friendship is out for me.

I'm a little subdued when we get to the actual interview questions, but I think I do well. Mrs. Fielding seems very positive by the time we wrap up. I'm not offered the job on the spot or anything, but she makes a point of informing me that a decision will be made in the upcoming weeks, and that she'll call me personally either way.

I leave feeling pretty good about things. But if I've learned anything from my experiences with Nolan, it's that you can't put all your eggs in one basket.

That's why when, several days later, I receive a call from the college recruitment center at my former school—about an entry-level marketing position at an ad agency in Chicago—I agree to fly across the country for an interview.

"Chicago? Wow, that's so far away," Aubrey murmurs when I bring her up to speed on my suddenly very active interview schedule.

"I know," I say, my eyes meeting hers. "I like being in the same city as you, but what can I do? I can't work at the casino forever."

"I know, Lain," she says softly.

She and I have just finished dinner. It's been just the two of us since Brent went away, but the team returns tomorrow. That means Brent will be back in town...and so will Nolan.

I need to talk to him to end things. He's still not communicated with me, and frankly I'm more than done now. Too bad I'll be halfway across the country when he returns. I guess I'll have to wait till I come back to speak with him. Or I could always take the coward's way out and text him my intentions to end things.

Maybe that'd be better, though. I wouldn't have to face him. But then again, if I move to Chicago I'll probably never face him again, as in I'll likely rarely, if ever, see him.

I swallow hard at the thought, and my eyes tear up.

"Lainey, are you all right?" Aubrey asks, moving to the chair next to me.

I force a smile. "I'm fine. I just have a lot to think about, you know?"

"Hey." She touches my forearm. "Are you sure about this interview in Chicago tomorrow? You really have to ask yourself if you'd truly be happy living all the way out there all alone?"

"You did it, and you were okay," I counter, reminding her of the job she held before she worked directly for the Wolves. "Your last position was based in Chicago. That's why you bought that townhouse you still hang onto."

"Yeah, yeah, you're right."

I suddenly remember something from a few weeks ago, a random talk she and I had about her selling her townhouse. I bring it up now.

"Hey, I just thought of something. Do you remember when you mentioned that you were seriously thinking about selling the townhouse? This was back a month or so ago."

"Yeah, I remember. Why?"

"Well, if you recall, I talked you out of it." She slowly nods, I guess remembering, and I go on to say, "Maybe I had a premonition or something. I mean, what I'm saying is it's a good thing you kept the townhouse. If I get the job, then I could live there, right?"

She smiles. "Of course, Lainey."

"See," I begin, mustering fake enthusiasm since I'm not really all that sure about a Chicago move. But that doesn't stop me from insisting, "That's one big thing already taken care of. It's like this is all weirdly meant to be."

Wow, clearly I'll grasp at anything to make myself leave Nolan. That's how badly I really don't want to go. I can tell Aubrey's not buying what I'm selling, but she refrains from saying as much.

Instead, she simply murmurs, "If you say so, Lainey."

"Why are you not excited?" I ask. Really, I'm asking myself.

Aubrey replies, "I am excited, sweetheart. It's just that I worry about you. Do you remember how lonely I was when I lived in Chicago? I don't want you to end up feeling that way."

I sigh. "It gets pretty lonely around here too, Aubs."

She just about floors me when she then asks, for the first time ever in a positive way, about Nolan. "What about Solvenson? I thought you two were close these days."

Okay, it's mostly positive. I could've worked with that too, perhaps gotten Aubrey on board with the idea of me and him. She's clearly softened on the guy. Too bad it's too late.

Since there's nothing left to lose, not anymore, I finally admit what I've been hiding for so long. "Nolan and I aren't going to work out, Aubs. Not as friends...or as anything else. We tried both ways, and neither worked, so it's over."

Her gaze meets mine. "I'm really sorry, Lainey."

"Yeah," I snort. "Thank you for saying that, but it looks like you were right about him all along."

"I wish I'd been wrong," she whispers, placing her hand over mine.

"Yeah, I wish you had been too. But you weren't, and, well, life goes on."

"Hey, listen," Aubrey says, tears in her eyes. "You can stay in my townhouse as long as you like. And I'll try to visit you as much as I can. Brent can stop by too, when he has games out there. And if you ultimately decide you like Chicago enough to stay permanently, I'll gift the freaking place to you. If you want it, that is."

I nod and thank her, but really all I want is Nolan, that damn stubborn man. If only Aubrey could "gift" him to me just as easily as she can the townhouse.

But she can't.

And like I told her, life must go on. Even if it is to be a life without Nolan.

21

AM I IN LOVE? IF SO, F*CK!

NOLAN

I come to a conclusion while I'm away, a potentially life-changing conclusion. Oddly enough, this revelation sneaks up on me during the game against the Winnipeg Jets, shortly after a power play where I score a goal.

The chain of events begins after Benny delivers a punishing, but still completely legal, check on one of the Jets forwards. Seconds later, that player retaliates by cross-checking Benny. That's not legal and a penalty is called. The Jets player is sent to the box, and the resulting Wolves power play is textbook perfection.

Brent's on the top power play unit with me, along with our second-line centerman, a dude named Jaxon Holland. Dylan Culderway is one of two defensemen on the ice, mostly because he's not only a great defenseman, but he has a killer shot from the point.

He takes that exact type of shot midway through the power play, but unfortunately the puck's on edge and careens away from the net. But the hockey gods smile down on us and send that wayward puck right to my stick.

Sometimes things work out like that.

Since I'm pretty much in front of the goal, not being covered well at all, I tap the puck past their goaltender and into the net.

Score!

The crowd quiets to an almost silence. No surprise there, as we are in Winnipeg. Nevertheless, I do hear a few scattered Wolves fans cheering here and there, but nothing of consequence. The lack of noise doesn't stop me and my teammates from celebrating on the ice.

Afterward, I return to the bench. There's roughly two minutes left to play, and I swear I feel like a new man. Maybe the universe has been smiling down on me all along.

Have I just been too dumb to see it?

I squirt some water in my mouth, spit it out, and think that possibility over. And then, again like there's some stronger force at work, I'm compelled to look up in the stands. That's when I swear I see Lainey.

My heart stills. It couldn't be her, could it? *No way.*

When I wipe away built-up moisture from inside my visor, I see it's just a girl who looks like Lainey. What really strikes me is how disappointed I am. How thinking, even just for a minute, that it was her had me feel good, *really* good, as in happy, a deep down in your bones kind of contentment, like when it's right it's right.

Holy hell, I think I know why—because I fucking love her!

How could I have been so blind all this time? Maybe I haven't been, though. I've kind of known for a while. That's why I've been fighting so hard all this time. I knew in my heart that Lainey Shelburne was the one who could alter my life. And despite my constant pushback, she has. I love her. And I finally know for sure, with no more lingering doubts, that I'm ready to give her more, much more. I'm ready to surrender my heart.

My stupid ass should have told Lainey all this after our encounter by the pool. But I left it in her hands again, which was me still trying to take the easy way out. Now I fully realize how wrong it was to fuck around and then keep my mouth shut.

Well, no more of that foolishness. Shit, I hope she'll still have me. I haven't called or texted, mostly because I haven't known what to say. But I sure know now.

The game ends then and the team files off the ice and into the locker room, with me bringing up the rear. I sit down on a bench in front of the stall I've been assigned. After I take off my helmet, I run my hand through my sweaty hair.

"You all right over there, Solvenson?" Dylan Culderway asks. He's at the stall next to mine.

"Yeah, man." I nod. "I'm good. Just thinking about some things, is all."

"I'll leave you to it, then."

"Thanks."

He turns away and continues to take off his gear, giving me the space I need to think this thing through. Like I said once before, Dylan and I are a lot alike. He knows when to leave a man alone to figure his shit out.

Speaking of which, where was I?

Ah, love and Lainey…

Do you definitely love her? a little voice in my head asks.

"Yeah, yeah, I do," I mutter. That's why I put in a good word for her with the head of marketing. Brent and Aubrey had done so already, but I once did Mrs. Fielding a huge favor by autographing a bunch of items she was auctioning off to raise money for a sick niece. That's why I knew encouraging words from me for Lainey would hold some weight with her.

Still, it's up to Lainey to prove herself worthy of the position. If she does gets the job, she'll stay in Las Vegas. We can move our relationship to the next level for sure then.

Wow, I can't believe I'm all-in on this. But I am. I'm ready to take the next step, finally.

I only hope it's not too late.

22

WOOHOO . . . NOT

LAINEY

The morning I'm at the airport, all set to fly to Chicago, I *finally* receive a text from Nolan.

"It's about time," I grumble, since this is the first I've heard from him since he went on the road with the team.

We need to talk, his text states. *I have something I need to tell you.*

I wonder what's weighing on him now. What could warrant this out-of-the-blue communication? Well, I sure have some things to say too!

Leaning back against the hard, uncomfortable back of the seat I'm perched on at the gate, I reply, *Yes, we sure do need to talk.*

He sends back, *I'll be home later this afternoon. Do you want to go to dinner? We can talk after.*

Hmm, "talk after" sounds like a euphemism for sex, so I can't help but roll my eyes. I can see the writing on the wall already. And I bet I can predict what he wants to tell me—that we should go right back to where we were, the good ole friend zone, but this new one we carved out, called "friends with benefits."

That's not really a friend zone, though, now is it? Nope, it's a place where boundaries are blurred and, worse yet, where I end up hurt by what can never be.

I don't think so, bud, I think. Oops. All fired up, I actually text that to him.

He shoots back *???*

Um, I just mean I can't go out with you tonight, I reply.

Why not?

I'm on my way out of town for an interview. I'm at the airport right now.

A pause, then, *where is this interview?*

Chicago.

A full minute passes, and then this pops up on the screen: *What happened with the interview with the Wolves?*

How do you know about that one?

A pause, then, *Brent told me.*

I sigh and inform him, *I haven't heard anything from the Wolves. And frankly, I'm sick and tired of waiting around for what-ifs and maybes. I have a life to live, Nolan. If I'm offered this job in Chicago, I'm taking it.*

Okay, that's a little harsh, and it's wrought with innuendo regarding our current situation. But it's the truth.

Nolan replies, *Good luck. I'm sure you'll do great. Anyone would be lucky to have you, Lainey.*

I swallow the lump in my throat as I read his clipped words, words that kill me with their lack of any real emotion. It's the same old closed-off Nolan, just a different day. Doesn't it bother him at all that I might be moving far, far away?

What does that say about me?

It says I'm a fool for allowing this to continue.

With tears in my eyes, I angrily stab at the phone, typing, *You know what, Nolan? I think no matter what happens with this interview it's time for you and me to go our separate ways.*

You're breaking up with me via text?

I bark out a bitter laugh and passengers stare over at me. I ignore them as I hastily—before I chicken out—text back, *We were never really ever together, remember?*

I guess you're right.

That's when I turn off the phone.

It really is over now.

Chicago in November is as cold outside as I feel inside.

After touching down, I do everything in a daze—collect my luggage from the baggage carousel, catch a cab from the airport to Aubrey's townhouse in Wicker Park, and let myself in her front door.

Dropping my bags on the floor, I give up on everything and trudge my tired ass upstairs to take a nap. First though, I have a really good cry. It's amazing how letting it all out can feel so good.

After sleeping for a few hours, I force myself back downstairs and trundle through the dining room.

And that's when I spy Al!

Al is an old stuffed animal from my childhood. A floppy green alligator who always makes me laugh, especially because of an ongoing inside joke with Aubrey. I'm glad she left him here sitting on a chair.

"Guess I should eat something, huh?" I mumble to Al, not caring if talking to an inanimate object makes me sound like I'm losing my mind. It's lonely being here alone. But I may as well get used to it. If I get the job, it'll be just me and Al spending *a lot* of alone-time together.

With that in mind, I say, "Hey, Al, let me go see what's in the pantry. I'll be right back."

After a mildly pathetic dinner of one-sided conversation with a stuffed animal, and eating PB&J on stale crackers—it was all I could find since I didn't feel like going grocery shopping or ordering takeout—I force myself to snap out of this ridiculous funk.

"I have an interview tomorrow," I tell Al. "I should be excited, right?"

Al, of course, does not reply, and I mutter, "Yeah, I feel pretty much the same way about things, little dude."

Despite my lack of enthusiasm, after I clear my plate, I fire up my laptop and begin diligently studying all the many notes I made about the ad agency on the flight to Chicago. I conclude early on that the job with the Wolves would be much more to my liking. I don't think I'm a big ad agency person, but now that Nolan and I are definitely through the best way for me to move *on* is to move *away*.

After reviewing my notes, I spend a quiet evening watching TV with Al. He even sleeps next to me, and the next day when I wake up, I tell him, "I wish I could bring you."

Since I obviously can't, I take a cab downtown for the interview on my own.

When I step out of the taxi, right away the wind blowing off the frozen lake just about freezes my cheeks to ice cubes. I tug the edges of the heavy wool scarf I dug from Aubrey's closet so I can cover my face as I walk to the office building where the interview's happening.

I swear I literally feel what little bit of color I had left from my day at Nolan's pool draining away with every step. Or maybe that's my enthusiasm. Whatever the case, when another gust of wind picks up, just as I reach the building, I hurry the hell in.

I'm still feeling blue, and all I can think is if I ace this interview and am offered the position, I don't know how I'll stand another Midwestern winter. The past few months of living in the desert have me totally spoiled. Or maybe I'm just realizing I much prefer the sun and heat. More likely, I just prefer a place where Nolan resides, even if we aren't together.

Does that make sense? No. I'm clearly losing it.

When I'm called in for the interview, I just kind of go through the motions. Funny, despite not caring all that much about the outcome, I still put on a good show. I guess since there's no pressure I appear relaxed, yet confident. At the end of the interview, I'm told I should expect to hear from someone shortly. Always a good sign, as my friends who've landed really good jobs have always been notified within twenty-four hours.

I should be elated, but I feel kind of blasé. I'm all like, *woohoo...not.* Consequently, I can't get out of Chicago fast enough.

I stop in at the apartment, grab my stuff, say *good-bye and I'll probably see you soon* to Al, and take a cab straight to the airport.

Back in Vegas, I receive a call from the ad agency the very next day.

They offer me the job.

Ah, my friends were right.

Since I've not heard anything from the Wolves, and I need a "real" job, now more so than ever to keep my mind off my in-shambles love life, I accept immediately.

The HR person is elated.

"Excellent," she says. "Can you be settled in and ready to start by the end of the month? We'd like you to start on December first."

Yikes, that's only three weeks away!

Why did I think I'd have more time? I guess because the Wolves position I interviewed for is still open. But this is the one that's being offered to me.

"Yes," I reply, decision made. "That's not a problem."

The phone call continues, with more details that I robotically jot down.

And then it's done and over, and my life has a new direction, just like that.

I have a career-oriented job.

And I'm moving away.

You have your whole life ahead of you, I remind myself.

Yeah, too bad it feels empty knowing Nolan will no longer be a part of it.

23

YOU GOTTA PLAY TO WIN

NOLAN

Lainey is really leaving, but I can't believe it.

It's happening, though, according to Brent. He showed up at my house yesterday and told me the news. I think he expected me to run straight down to his house and beg Lainey not to go.

Why else would he make a point of stopping by?

But what did I do? Nothing. I just stood there, nodding and acting like it was all okay.

Brent looked disappointed when he left.

Hell, I get it. I'm disappointed with myself. But this isn't about me. Sure, I *want* to stop Lainey from moving away, particularly now that I've admitted to myself that I love her. But I just can't do that to her. It's *because* of the love I feel for her that I can't, in good conscience, keep her from pursuing her dreams. She wanted to find a career position, one where she could put to use the degree she worked so hard for, and this is her chance.

I won't stand in her way. It'd be like if the team were to make another Cup run, and Lainey asked me not to play. Yeah, not fair. Not fair at all. Still, doing the right thing doesn't mean it doesn't hurt like fucking hell. I finally opened my heart to Lainey, and to love, and she doesn't even fucking know it.

Now she never will.

I'm so miserable I decide to do what Brent did when Aubrey left him last year—I immerse myself in hockey. But even that doesn't help. Sure, I rack up more assists and a few goals, thus setting some personal and professional records, but even those milestones feel hollow.

On one particularly lonely night, I get wind that Dylan and Benny are hitting up the town.

What the hell, I think, *I should just join them.*

And I do. We grab dinner at a trendy, upscale restaurant, and then head to the Strip to gamble a little. Benny's been on a winning streak lately with blackjack, so we let him pick which casino we should go to first.

He chooses Planet Hollywood, where we all hit big. Of course, we're throwing down lots of money. You gotta play to win, right?

"Which place is calling to you now?" Dylan asks Benny as we leave PH with full wallets.

Tourists and fellow gamblers push by, but we ignore them as we wait for Lucky Benny to make his next selection.

"Yeah," I reiterate to him, "next stop is totally your call."

Benny frowns as he peers up and down the Strip. The colorful neon lights flash off his stubbled face and blond hair as he thinks it over.

"Any day now," I mumble, feeling impatient when five minutes go by with no decision made.

"Greatness takes time," Benny shoots back.

"Yeah," Dylan chimes in, frowning over at me. "Just let him think it over, man."

"All right, all right, all right," I say, sounding a lot like Matthew McConaughey.

Finally, Benny makes a decision. "I got a strong feeling about one place in particular." He shoots me a sidelong glance. "But, dude, you're so not gonna like it."

"Aw, fuck." I sense where this is heading. The casino where Lainey works is directly across the street. And that's the one Benny can't keep his damn eyes off of.

"Hey, it doesn't have to be that one," he says, sending me a look filled with apology for even mentioning it. "We can just go somewhere else. My hot streak is due to end soon anyway."

"Whoa, hey, I don't know about that," Dylan counters. He gestures back to where we just cleaned up. "We walked away with some stellar winners at this place."

I can't argue with sound logic. Besides, I'm not a pussy. Gesturing over to Lainey's place of employment, or rather her place of employment until she leaves for her real job—and her new life without me—I say, "Let's just head over. It's fine."

"Are you sure?" both guys ask at the same time.

"I am," I assure them. "Lainey may not even be working tonight." I have no clue since we've had no contact, so I add, "Even if she is, it's not a problem. We'll be busy playing cards, eh?"

"True," Benny concurs.

"So are we doing this or what?" Dylan says impatiently.

I know he firmly believes in confronting things head-on. I bet if he knew the extent of my feelings for Lainey, he'd tell me to quit being such a stubborn prick and just fucking lay my heart out on the table. He'd say Lainey should have all the facts before she leaves. He doesn't believe in allowing an obstacle to hold you back. His philosophy is you grab hold of that motherfucker and *make* it move out of your way. Or die trying.

I don't disagree, on principle, but I can't mess up Lainey's life. I'm afraid she'll base her entire decision on the fact that I've come around. Her heart is so good, and I know she loves me just as much as I love her, even though we've never said the words.

Still, I'd hate if someday she looked at me with those beautiful turquoise eyes and they were filled with resentment. That could happen if I swoop in at the last minute and derail her new life.

That's also why I won't call Mrs. Fielding and press the issue with the Wolves. If she wants to call Lainey and offer her the job, she'll do so. And this way if she does, it'll be because Lainey is the best candidate for the job. Not because one of their star players intervened.

Helping Lainey secure a job interview is one thing, but using my influence to change the course of her life? I just won't do that. Even Brent and Aubrey stop short of going that far.

"So…" I blow out a breath and make the first move to cross the street. "Who's feeling lucky tonight?"

24

THIS JOB CAN'T END SOON ENOUGH

LAINEY

Only three more shifts, including the one I'm working, and then my life as a cocktail waitress will blissfully end.

The timing couldn't be better, and this shift can't end soon enough. The crowds seem especially crazy tonight. Maybe it's due to the upcoming Thanksgiving holiday, I don't know. What I do know is everyone is drinking more than usual, more belligerent than ever, and pawing at us waitresses like there's some kind of contest.

"I swear," I grind out after escaping one handsy customer. I'm back at the drink well with another waitress, Penny, who's been experiencing the same thing all night. "If one more pervert tries to grab my ass, they're going to wear their next cocktail."

"I hear ya, sweetie," Penny replies. She's in her early thirties, and as she tells it, has been here three years going on what feels like fifty. "Just be happy *you're* done for good after this weekend."

"Trust me, I'm elated," I reply, chuckling as I place three drinks—two rum and cokes and one soda water—an order that came in through our automated system for table 22—on a tray. "I'm so over this place."

"Amen to that," Penny says. "Now keep that in mind, and get back out there in the trenches."

"Yes, sir," I tease, turning to go.

As I start out to table 22, she calls out to me, "Promise not to forget about us little people once you're a certified ad guru and raking in the big bucks."

"That will never happen," I yell back over my shoulder. "I promise I'll come back and leave the biggest tips ever!"

"Ooh, I'll let you grab my ass for sure if you do that," I hear her teasingly retort before I'm out of earshot.

She's such a sweetheart, always making me laugh. In fact, I'm smiling big and wide when I reach table 22.

And then I'm suddenly not.

"Oh," I mutter dejectedly.

At table 22 sits the one man I never expected to show up at my place of employment.

"Hello, Lainey," a smooth voice replies—Nolan's smooth voice.

I set down his drink, one of the rum and cokes, in front of him. He seems equal parts surprised and pleased to see me. He's also managing to somehow exude über suaveness and sophistication. But then again, that's always him.

I'm so captured by Nolan—partly because I haven't seen him since our day by the pool, and partly because I'm always like this around him—that I barely notice Benny and Dylan are there too. But when Benny clears his throat, I give him and Dylan a quick *hey*.

Then I return to checking out Nolan.

He looks exceptional, his dark hair slicked back and his blue eyes burning pure ice. He's wearing a black suit, red tie, and a white button-down shirt. And though his attire screams business magnate to the unaware, the cut of his clothes can't hide his powerful, athletic body, a body made for performance—in more areas than just hockey, as I well know.

I swallow hard as I force back memories of Nolan working his body over mine, taking me, making me his.

"Lainey?" He cocks his head. "Are you okay?"

"I'm fine," I snap, though clearly I'm not.

If I were *fine*, I wouldn't be standing there gawking at the man, thinking about sex with him.

What is *wrong* with me? I should be acting all cool and aloof toward him, seeing as I broke things off.

And with damn good reason! I remind myself.

Pulling my shit together, I straighten my spine and focus on the other two guys. We exchange more pleasantries as I finally pass out their drinks. Nolan, at one point, asks for a cocktail napkin. I hold one out to him, but make no eye contact. I just keep on chatting away with Benny and Dylan, ignoring Mr. I Suddenly Need Something From You, Lainey—albeit just a napkin.

Clearly miffed by my sudden blasé attitude toward him, he says, "We can ask for another waitress, if that'd make you feel more comfortable." His hand brushes against mine as he slips the napkin from my grasp.

I try not to feel so affected by his touch, but the truth is I am. "That won't be necessary," I snap.

Damn it, I'm determined to do this.

"We'll be moving over to one of the game tables soon, anyway," Benny says gently, gesturing to a nearby blackjack pit.

"Really, it's not a problem," I maintain. "In fact, I can bring your next round to wherever you are."

Benny opens his mouth to reply, but I never get to hear what he was about to say. An obnoxious drunk, one I'd hoped had left, calls over to me from a few tables away.

"Hey, waitress," he slurs. "You think you can wiggle that cute little ass over here sometime soon? I'd really like to place another drink order before next year."

Nolan visibly bristles. "Is that asshole bothering you? Just say the word, Lainey, and I'll take care of it."

I'd actually love that, but I can't involve him in my work problems. We're nothing to each other anymore. Plus, he has the team and his reputation to think of. Even though no one is actively bugging any of the guys for autographs, people have been glancing over and whispering.

Shaking my head, I tell Nolan, "No, I got this."

Dylan leans in and quietly asks, "You sure, hon?"

His rich brown eyes tell me he means business. I'm not surprised. Nolan once told me Dylan's mom died at the hands of a violent, abusive man. Not surprisingly, Dylan doesn't take too kindly to men disrespecting women in any way.

I'm reminded of what Brent told me about these guys having my back. I have no doubt that Dylan would throw down right alongside Nolan. Benny too, based on the daggers he's shooting Dickhead's way.

It feels good to have these men so willing to back me up, but I assure them, "Everything's under control. This is why we have bouncers." I don't add that I currently don't see one nearby.

I return my gaze to Nolan, and wait… Is that disappointment on his face? Does he actually *want* to kick someone's ass for me? Wow, I think he does. There's a certain bygone chivalry in that. Still, it doesn't matter. He and I are through when it comes to love, which means there's no need for him to defend me.

I walk away from table 22, take a deep breath, and head over to take Dickhead's order.

25

LISTEN TO YOUR HEART

NOLAN

I swear there are times when I wish I wasn't a well-known hockey player. Like right now. If I didn't have an image to uphold, which the team mandates, I'd hustle my ass over to the table where Lainey's currently taking an order and promptly hoist the short, paunchy dude who's been giving her a hard time all night up off his stool so I can kick his ass six ways to Sunday.

"Don't do it, Solvenson." Dylan gives me that look, one that tells me he knows exactly where my head's at.

"Shit," I bite out, since he's right.

But when he sees I can't stop fuming, he changes course. "If it is going to happen, it needs to be discreet."

"Where're you thinking?" I ask, quirking a brow. "That little prick has been saying shit to Lainey all night. Every time she's over at his table, bringing an order or taking a new one, it's obvious he's giving her crap."

"I noticed that too," Benny chimes in, shaking his head. "It's really fucked-up."

"It sure is," I agree. "That's why I'm definitely going to have some kind of a little 'talk' with him before the night is over."

Benny knows what I really mean, and says, "Hey, I'm in. I have some things to say to him too."

"Yeah, me too," Dylan, not surprisingly, chimes in.

I'm appreciative my teammates are with me off the ice, as well as on. "Good, then we're in agreement that he's going to get a lesson on how *not* to treat your cocktail waitress."

"Or any woman," Dylan says in a low voice.

"Now we just have to wait for the right time."

We head back over to the blackjack table, where a new hand's about to be dealt. My mind remains on Lainey, however, even as I take a seat.

Fuck, I'll be so glad when she's done with this place.

Yet another reason why I *must* keep my true feelings for her under wraps. When I first saw her tonight, as she was approaching our table with our tray of drinks, I went from shock that she was actually working *and* assigned to our table—what's the chance?—to complete joy. I wanted nothing more than to grab her up in my arms and share with her that I fucking *love* her!

But I quickly composed myself.

And good thing I did, since Lainey needs to move on now more than ever. If for no other reason than to get away from smarmy pricks like the one she's been putting up with tonight.

Over the next hour, the blackjack table is good to us. Our chips keep multiplying. I make sure to keep an eye on Lainey, though. Luckily, the dickhead bugging her seems to have backed off. It's probably because there's a security guy hanging around now.

Dylan pulls me from my thoughts when he says, "Benny sure was right about this casino." Turning to the man in question, he adds, "You have a knack indeed, my friend, for picking the winning spots."

"I guess I do," Benny agrees. "The streak is strong tonight."

And it is, as we all win at least once the next several hands. We cash out shortly thereafter, collect our winnings, and return to table 22 in the cocktail lounge. But I notice when we order a final round of drinks from Lainey that she seems troubled.

Fuck the fact that we're not together anymore. I gently touch her arm. "Did something more happen with that dickhead?" I shoot his table a killer look. Too bad he's not looking my way.

She shakes her head, but kind of leans into me, like she suddenly needs my protection.

Suddenly, like a thunderbolt hitting me, I get this overwhelming feeling that time is running out. But is the feeling regarding us…or something else?

I know then that I better figure this shit out fast. She's leaving soon. Like, for good. But for now I check again that she's all right.

"Yes, Nolan," she insists, "everything's under control. The bouncer had a long talk with that guy."

"Did it help?"

"Mostly." She looks away, but before I can ask for elaboration, she quickly adds, "It doesn't matter. My shift's ending soon, anyway."

I blow out a relieved breath. "Well, that's good. We're heading out soon too. We can walk you to your car."

"Oh, that's not necessary, Nolan."

I'm having none of that. Lainey's told me in the past that she parks in the underground garage's employee section. Apparently, that area is dimly lit and can feel desolate, not unlike most parking garages. That would all be bad enough, but factor in the asshole that's had it out for her all night, and let's just say I don't like it one bit.

That's why I press the matter. But Lainey insists she's fine to walk on her own.

"No, we're coming with you," I counter, despite her protestations. "And that's the final word."

"Nolan." She pins me with an aggravated look, and then hisses, "You're making this into a production. Can you just stop already?"

"Okay, okay." I give in, but only after I check the prick's table and see he's slipped out. Too bad any chance of me and the boys following through on our little "talk" with him is gone.

Lainey looks like she's about to say something more to me, but just then one of her coworkers calls her over to ask her a question. When she returns with our drinks, she doesn't seem irritated with me anymore and proceeds to inform me, "Hey, I'm sorry I snapped at you. It was actually sweet that you wanted to walk me out. But you definitely don't have to. I won't be alone. Penny just told me she's leaving soon too. I'll head down to the garage with her as soon as she's done."

I still don't like it, but I don't push. I take solace in the fact that the prick's long gone. Maybe he drank too much and is puking his guts out somewhere. I hope so, since it'd serve him right.

The guys and I close out our tab shortly thereafter and, after saying goodbye to Lainey, head out.

All the while, though, something urges me to turn back, to go check on her just to be sure.

26

RESCUE ME

LAINEY

Penny is delayed, and it sucks. I'm beat from this crazy night and just want to go home. I could wait for her, but come on. I've gone down to the parking garage alone without incident dozens of times. I'm always fine, and I'm sure tonight will be no exception.

So, I say good-bye to Penny. She apologizes for getting hung up, but I tell her, "No worries."

I then head down to the parking garage. When I step out of the elevator, three levels below ground, everything looks the same as it always does. For some reason, though, I feel uneasy.

"Oh, stop. You're just freaking yourself out over nothing." Despite my positive affirmations, I still walk briskly to my car, listening to the occasional rumble of cars moving along on the next level up. "See, just the usual sounds of the night. It's all good."

I start to relax as I turn a corner and spot my car.

Almost there.

Looking down, I start digging around in my purse for the key fob to unlock the door. But suddenly, just as my fingers are wrapping around the familiar rectangular edge, I hear heavy footsteps coming up from behind me.

Spinning around, wishing I had mace in my hand instead of a harmless plastic key fob, I'm confronted with…no one.

"Is somewhere there?" I call out when there's a shuffling noise from behind a wide support pole.

There's no response, so I venture, "Penny, is that you?"

No answer again, except for a *drip-drip* of a leaky pipe in the background.

Stupid over-active imagination!

Turning back to continue to my car, I let out a relieved breath. But still, in the interest of being smart about things, I pick up the pace. If I'd really been smart, I would've waited for Penny.

Suddenly, out of the corner of my eye, I detect movement from my right. And then, before it even really registers, a dark figure—a man—rushes toward me.

"What the—" I am knocked me off my feet, and the key fob goes flying.

I jerk my head up and am confronted with the person who just put me on my ass. "Shit."

"Shit is right, dumb bitch."

I shouldn't be surprised that it's the short, flabby asshole that was harassing me all freaking night. And, unfortunately for me, he doesn't look so small anymore. No, not with the way he's looming over me with his creepy grin holding no hint of any misplaced humor in having knocked me to the ground.

But I refuse to give him the satisfaction of cowering. I defiantly stand up, mumbling to myself, "What a dickhead."

"What did you just say?" said dickhead growls out.

I ignore him, and get to walking away as fast as I can. Each step in the direction of my car feels like a mile, I'm that fucking scared. And I have good reason—my assailant is following me.

I break into a run, but I don't get far. Dickhead slams into me, shoving my body up against a random SUV.

"I asked you a question, you stupid slut," he grinds out as spittle that reeks of booze showers my cheek.

I don't call him a *dickhead* again. I just start yelling for help and trying to get away. Too bad no one is around.

"Get the fuck off me," I scream when he thwarts every effort I make to escape.

I put up a valiant struggle when he tries to press my body to the SUV, but he still succeeds in caging me in. *God, I can't think about what's coming next.* I just keep kicking and shoving and clawing and calling for help.

"Quit fighting me!" he screams, slamming me back against the SUV. "And shut the fuck up!"

I keep struggling to escape, and yelling, until he backhands me.

Oh my God.

I can't even catch my breath. This must be what it feels like to have the wind knocked out of you. I slump forward since he's stepped back. I place my hands on my knees, until finally, I can breathe again. Sucking in big gulps of air, I lean back against the SUV, randomly wondering who it belongs to and wishing whoever it is would show up right about now.

Clearly, I'm no match for this drunken bastard. And I don't know what he has in store for me. Or maybe I do, and I just don't want to face it, seeing as his nasty fingers are now toying with the ties on my corset.

When I let out a scared squeak, he leans in and says, "Keep quiet, and I won't hurt you too much."

Bile rises in my throat and, since I can't seem to find my voice, I whisper, "You don't want to do this."

He laughs. "Yeah, actually I do."

"Please. If you leave right now, I swear I won't tell anyone what happened."

It's not true, and he knows it.

Without warning, he grabs my face and squeezes so hard that my lips pucker up all clown-like. "That mouth never quits, does it?" he sneers.

With his free hand, he begins to unzip his pants. "Good thing I have something that's going to keep you quiet for a while."

I start shaking my head, despite his hold on my face. He lets go enough to force me to my knees, which is worse. That's when I start crying. He's still limp, thank God, but he's trying to rectify the situation.

I can't escape. He has me trapped between him and the SUV. I never thought I'd end up like this. But then, suddenly, my assailant is pulled away by two big bodies. No wait, make that three.

I slide all the way to the ground and wipe away the tears that are clouding my vision. I need to see who has come to my rescue.

"Oh," I breathe out when I see three guys—Benny, Dylan, and my knight in shining armor, Nolan.

I murmur his name, but then the events of the night catch up to me and I slowly lose consciousness.

27

I SHOULD KILL THE BASTARD

NOLAN

It takes Benny and Dylan together to pull me off the drunken douchebag who dared to attack my girl.

"Stop it, man! You're going to kill him."

"That's the fucking idea," I hiss out between clenched teeth as Benny slips between me and the prick I'm doling out punches on. The bastard is barely fighting back, and Benny is able to separate us by shoving me back against a cement pole before I go too far.

"Calm down, Nolan," he says.

Up to this point, I've seen nothing but red—the colors of rage, hatred, and anger. But now that I'm away from the situation, albeit by only a few feet, my mind clears enough to realize I've yet to check on Lainey.

I divert my attention over to where she's on the ground, slumped against an SUV. Dylan is crouched down next to her, checking her vitals.

Fuck, she's out cold.

"Let me go," I say softly to Benny. He knows quiet me is far scarier than fired-up me, and he releases me immediately.

Ignoring the fuck rolling around on the concrete—he's no longer an issue—I go to Lainey. When I drop to my knees next to her Dylan makes room for me.

"We should call an ambulance," he says. "He hit her in the face pretty hard."

I reach out and tentatively touch her rapidly swelling cheek. Tossing a glare over my shoulder to where Benny is currently guarding her assailant so he doesn't get up and run off, I state in the same dangerously quiet voice as before, "I should make him pay for this."

"I think you already have."

"I mean more."

Dylan blows out a breath. "Let the authorities handle it from here on out, Nolan. He's not worth it. You have a career to think of." He nods to Lainey, who's coming to, and adds, "And more importantly, you have her."

Lainey starts to come to and, running my fingers through my hair, I say, "Yeah, you're right."

Dylan calls the police then, and after they arrive we are all interviewed. No one asks about the injuries on the bad guy. I don't know if it's because we're well-known hockey players and the police are cool with keeping our involvement on the down-low, or if there's some other reason. We find out it's the latter. Seems Lainey's not the first cocktail waitress this jackass has lain in wait for.

"It could've been much worse, Miss Shelburne," one of the officers informs her.

She shivers in my arms. That's right, I haven't let go of her since she woke up. I even insisted on staying by her side when she gave her statement to the police. But now there's a lady officer who wants to speak with Lainey alone, and also have her checked over by the paramedics who arrived shortly after the officers.

"S'okay, Nolan," she tells me when I hesitate to let her go. She pats my forearm, like she's consoling me. "I'll be fine."

Logic tells me she will be, but my heart urges me to never let her out of my sight again.

She's leaving for Chicago soon, asshole. How do you plan on keeping an eye on her then?

"Good question," I murmur.

"What's that?" Lainey says.

"It's nothing, babe." I tug her closer, kiss her uninjured cheek, and then reluctantly let her go. "Go talk to the officer and get checked out. But when you're done, there are some things we need to talk about, things that can no longer wait." *She needs to know I love her. Fuck holding off.*

She eyes me curiously. "Like what kinds of things?"

Like how much I love you, I hope my eyes convey.

But since Lainey's not a mind reader, she has no idea. She's going to need to *hear* the words, and that means *all* the words.

Good thing I'm finally ready to say them all…and more.

28

LAST NIGHTS AND LOST WORDS

LAINEY

Turns out I don't need to go to a hospital. I mean, I'm told I probably should, but I insist I'm okay. The paramedics still examine me and give me ice for my swollen cheek. And then I'm free to leave.

Benny and Dylan go their separate ways, but I decide to let Nolan take me home. I figure I can pick up my car tomorrow. I'm too shaken to drive, plus Nolan mentioned that we need to talk.

I don't want to get into an in-depth conversation in front of Brent and Aubrey's place, so when we reach the house, and he slows down, I say, "Can we just go to your house? I'd rather not have to explain my swollen cheek to Aubrey…or Brent."

"Of course we can just go there," he says, driving on.

We don't say much more the next minute or two, but after we pull into his garage and the door goes down, he tells me, "Just so you don't worry, I already told Dylan and Benny not to say a word about what happened tonight, especially not to Brent. Not that they would, but I figured I'd mention it just in case."

I really appreciate his discretion, and I have no problem expressing my gratitude. Reaching over and squeezing his hand, I say, "Thanks, Nolan."

When we're finally in the house, I realize I feel more at home here than I do at my sister and her fiancé's place. Maybe it's because the longer I stay at Brent and Aubrey's, the more I feel like an outsider. There's no denying I'm a third wheel in their close relationship. It's different here at Nolan's, especially after what happened tonight. Things feel exceptionally right, like it's finally just me and him, united at last.

"How're you feeling?" he asks.

"Not too bad, but a little tired."

He nods and leads me into the living room, where he helps me settle in on his comfy sofa. "That better?" he asks.

"Much."

He covers me with a soft knit blanket, then steps back and says, "Let me run upstairs and find you something to wear. I imagine you'd be more comfortable in different clothes, eh?"

"Yes," I murmur, happy to let him take care of me like this. "I definitely would."

He leaves, and a few minutes later he returns with a pair of gray lounge pants and a thick Wolves sweatshirt. As he hands me the items, I again thank him.

"You don't have to keep thanking me, Lainey." He checks my ice pack, and finding it mostly melted, he says, "I'll be back in a minute, I'm going to grab you a fresh pack from the freezer."

I don't thank him this time, I just say "okay" before he heads to the kitchen.

While he's gone, I change into the fresh clothes. Since they belong to him, and are much too large, I have to roll up the legs of the pants like seven times. The sweatshirt literal hangs on me once I have that on. I don't care. It just feels good to have the work clothes off, seeing as I couldn't stop feeling that disgusting guy's thick fingers on me, untying my corset. Shuddering, I kick the offending garment under the coffee table.

Nolan, returning with the ice pack, catches me and says, "You're done with that place for good I hope. You weren't thinking of working your final shifts, were you?"

I shake my head vehemently. "Hell, no. Not after what happened tonight."

He breathes a sigh of relief, and then takes a seat next to me. Gently, he presses the fresh, and I notice towel-wrapped ice pack to my cheek.

His blue eyes convey deep concern as he murmurs, "I think it's wise to *never* go back there."

I lean into his touch and close my eyes. "There'd be no point, anyway. I'm leaving for Chicago soon."

"About that, Lainey…"

I open my eyes, and he reaches out to stroke my hair. It feels so good to be taken care of by Nolan. When he lets go like this, he has a way of making you feel like you're the most important person in his life.

If only that were really true. Maybe then I wouldn't go to Chicago. The last thing I want to do after what just went down is to start all over somewhere else, completely alone.

I sigh, and Nolan starts to say something. But I don't want this moment ruined by words. Or rather, by the lack of the ones I long to hear.

"Shhh…" I place a finger to his lips. "Don't say anything. Not right now, okay? I know you mentioned that we need to talk, but whatever it is you want to say it can wait for later."

Truth is I'm afraid all he wants to tell me is his final goodbye. I think he's ready to send me off into the world and let go of what we had…and all that might have been.

And I'm just not ready for that. Not now…and maybe not ever.

He gives me a sad smile. "Sure, Lainey, we can talk later. Go ahead and rest for now."

When he opens his arms, nodding for me to crawl into them, I do so without hesitation. I wedge the ice pack between his chest and my cheek, and then I close my eyes and think how this is probably my last night with Nolan Solvenson.

29

ALL THE WORDS

NOLAN

Words. What are they, anyway? When you think about it, they're nothing more than letters strung together, that when uttered make a certain sound. Funny how impactful those sounds can be, though. It always amazes me how words can hurt or soothe, heal sometimes, or rip you to shreds.

Sometimes not saying them at all speaks volumes, as well.

That's what I've done too much of the time. And look where it's gotten me too—alone...or about to be.

I hold Lainey close. I don't want to lose her, not tonight or any night. I'd like to hold her like this for hours, but I feel moisture from her ice pack seeping through my shirt.

I move the pack aside and turn her head to assess the damage to her cheek. Lainey's sleeping so soundly that my movements don't rouse her one bit. Her cheek is red, but the swelling is down considerably.

Sighing, I shift beneath her so I can stretch my long legs. I'm clad in a pair of lounge pants like the ones I loaned her, only mine aren't hanging on me.

Once I have my back propped up against the sofa arm, I ease her down to rest against me, with her injured cheek facing up.

She stirs at last, mumbling my name along with a contented sigh.

"I love you," I reply without thinking.

I expect to feel panic at this inadvertent omission, but I don't. In fact, it feels good to say those words to her, even if she is sleeping. It's what I planned to tell her tonight, anyway.

Well, the words are out there now, for better or for worse. If only she knew the power they hold to break me. Because I *mean* those words—I fucking love Lainey Shelburne.

I say them again, a little more forcefully. "I love you, Lainey." *Damn, putting it out there feels good.*

I'm thinking she's asleep still, but I quickly realize she's not when I hear her breath catch in her throat.

Shit, she heard me.

How do I feel about that?

Terrified slightly, but mostly relieved.

She lifts her head from my chest and stares up at me, bleary-eyed but more coherent than she's been since the attack.

"What did you just say?" she murmurs.

"I...uh..." I touch her cheek. It's a little redder than it was moments ago, but maybe that's because she's a little flushed now. "We should get you more ice," I quietly state.

Yeah, deflecting is my go-to defense, even when I don't want it to be. Good thing Lainey's having none of it.

Smacking my hand away, she says, "Screw the ice. I want to hear what I think you just said."

"If you heard me the first time, I don't see why I need to say it again—"

"Nolan..." Her tone is a warning.

I gaze down at her, into those expressive turquoise eyes. What *is* holding me back? Nothing, as I'm no longer afraid.

So I just say it again, "I love you."

Despite the sincerity in my tone, she peers up at me, disbelieving.

Wow, have I really been so bad that she doesn't trust what I'm saying? I was right that words—or lack thereof—have consequences. But I do love her, and I'm willing to spend the rest of my life proving it to her. "If that's what it takes," I murmur to myself.

She eyes me curiously, and I go on to explain everything to her. I share not only what I was just thinking, but also all my fears, all my regrets, and the many things I've thought about lately.

"So *this* is what you wanted to talk about?" she queries.

"Yes."

"I never would've guessed."

"Yeah, I bet."

We both share a chuckle at that, but then she softly inquires, "Why now? Is it because of what happened earlier tonight?"

I take a deep breath and think that over. Is my wanting to talk to her now because of what happened? I don't unequivocally know, but I try to explain what I'm thinking as best as I can.

"I guess tonight *did* spur me on," I admit. "It certainly made me realize one thing."

"What's that?"

"When you love someone—with all your heart, like I do you—you need to let them know."

She smiles, but then I have a burst of panic and I share it with her. "What if something worse"—I shudder—"would've happened and I'd never had the chance to tell you I love you?"

"Nolan, stop torturing yourself. I'm fine." I raise a brow as I nod to her cheek, and she amends, "Well, more or less fine."

We sit then for a minute, soaking that in, until she asks softly, "How long have you kept all this inside, Nolan? How long have you known your true feelings?"

"For about a couple of weeks now—"

"Wait, what?" She sits up, crawls over into my lap, straddles me, then proceeds to smack her hands down, hard, on my chest. "You've knows for a couple of *weeks*?"

"Ow. And yes."

"And you were just going to sit around and let me tromp off to Chicago none the wiser?"

"That was the plan."

"For what crazy reason would you do that?"

I place my hands over hers. They're still on my chest, but thankfully not in smacking mode anymore.

I blow out a breath, and then confess, "I didn't want to fuck up your life any more than I already have. After jerking you around for months, which I feel pretty shitty about now, it didn't seem fair for me to ride in on some imaginary white horse and whisk you away. Not when things were finally happening for you on the career front."

She rolls her eyes. "Fuck the career, Nolan."

"Don't say that, Lainey. It's your dream."

She laughs. "No, it's really not." She stills, and her eyes bore into mine as she then tells me, "*You're* my dream, Nolan. And before you say anything, I don't care how antiquated that may sound. Feelings and relationships are always going to mean more to me than jobs and careers. It's just how I'm wired. Sure, I want to find a decent position, but a career, for me, will never be the end-all, be-all of my existence. Love will always mean more than some stupid job."

I don't know if that means she's staying, but I need to find out. For now, though, I'm stuck on one part of what she said—the "love" part.

"So…are you saying you love me too?" I softly inquire.

Fuck, can she hear how vulnerable I am right now? I don't care if she does. She can rip out my heart and stomp all over it, if she's so inclined. I thought I was in love a long time ago, with the woman who did me wrong, but I realize now that that was some immature version of love. The pain my ex-wife caused me was due more to humiliation than a true broken heart.

Lainey, however, could truly destroy me, simply by not loving me back. Though I don't think she's leaning that way. No, Miss Shelburne is looking at me with more love in her eyes than I deserve.

"Yes," she says. "I love you, you silly, stubborn man."

"I may be stubborn, that's true," I concede. And then it's time to lighten things up. "But," I continue, placing my hands on her hips and pressing her down to a part of me that is always hard for her—"does *that* feel silly to you?"

Closing her eyes, she lets out a little moan.

"Mmm, no," she rasps as she grinds down on me. "Not one bit silly, at all."

30

ECSTASY, AND NOT THE DRUG

LAINEY

I want Nolan, more than I ever have in the past. And that's saying a lot, since I pretty much burn for the man constantly.

Nonetheless, because of what happened earlier in the night, and before things go too far, he pauses, hands stilling my hips as he asks, "Are you sure about this?"

I drag his long-sleeved tee up his firm, smooth chest. "Lift," I command. He complies and I make short work of his shirt, tossing it aside. "And to answer your question, I've never been surer of anything in my life."

I mean, we just declared our love for one another! I *need* to be with him.

So, I tug my Wolves sweatshirt up over my head and unsnap my bra, freeing my breasts. Nolan can't tear his gaze away. He loves my boobs. But even better, he freaking loves *me*.

Reaching up, he reverently cups one mound, then the other. He shifts beneath me as he does, stilling when he's lined up perfectly against me.

With only thin lounge pants separating us, I can feel freaking *everything*, prompting me to groan, "You always feel so amazing."

"So do you."

God, Nolan's voice, his urgent but gentle touch, I love this man so much. I need him closer, as in, as close as two people can get.

Lying down on him, chest to chest, I press our bare torsos together. "You're so warm," he whispers.

"You are too."

We stop moving then and just *feel*. He wraps his arms around me, like he may lose me, and tells me again, "I love you."

"I love you too...so very, very much."

"I want you," he says softly, "but I don't want to rush things tonight."

"Me neither."

Between sweet kisses peppered across my jaw, and then down my neck, he murmurs, "Let me just love you slowly like this."

"Yes."

Nolan holds me then for what feels like forever, kissing me softly, in a way that makes me feel so alive. I explore Nolan's mouth with my tongue, while skimming my hands over every part of his body that's within reach. And though everything is done slowly, somewhere along the line the rest of our clothes are discarded, leaving me able to, at last, grasp him in my hands.

Yes, *hands*. Nolan is so damn big that two hands are necessary to *really* grab hold of him.

"I love this part of you too," I say, leaning back, my smile coy.

He shoots me back a sly smile of his own. "It clearly loves you too."

I laugh. "God, you're so sexy when you smile like that. You just look so genuinely happy."

"*You* make me happy," he says. But then his grin turns wicked and I know we're back to teasing when he adds, "And I promise you I'm not just saying that because you're holding my cock."

"Hmm, I don't believe you at all," I purr as I start stroking him slowly.

He rasps back, "Yeah, I'll admit you holding my dick...and definitely you stroking it like that"—he inhales a sharp breath when I squeeze—"are definitely helping to up my happiness level significantly."

"In that case, I think we can do one better, Mr. Solvenson."

"Oh yeah? How's that?"

Leaning down until the head of his cock is pressed to my lips, I peer up and say, "What about now? How are those happiness levels faring?"

"Shit, Lainey, we may be reaching off-the-chart levels of ecstasy now."

"May be? Hell, Nolan, I say we do."

Before he can say another word, I take him in my mouth. I'm pretty sure then that off-the-charts levels of ecstasy are most definitely achieved.

31

SHE NEVER SAW THAT ONE COMING

NOLAN

Off-the-chart levels of ecstasy are definitely achieved. But that's not my finest moment. No, my highest state of bliss doesn't occur when she's taking me in her mouth—though shit, that does feel pretty damn amazing. But the true bliss occurs when I'm sinking into her and feeling all her warmth and, more importantly, all her love.

Afterward, while we're resting I soak in the moment, and I am so damn happy. The only thing that breaks me from my happy state is when Lainey mentions how she wishes she could hide out for a day or two.

"Why?" I ask, concerned.

"I just don't want to go home and have to explain the bruise on my face." She sighs. "Aubrey worries enough about me already, and Brent's sure to wonder how I got hurt."

"So stay here," I offer. "I'll go with Benny later to get your car and take it to their house. I'll tell your sister that you're staying with me for a couple of days."

"Wow, she's going to wonder. She thinks we're through."

"Eh..." I shrug. "Your sister had a ton of back-and-forth with Brent. I think she'll understand."

"Maybe," Lainey replies. "But are you definitely sure it's okay for me to stay here?"

Lainey's worried I'll get weird, but she needn't. I'm past that...I think. I guess we'll see, but I say to her, "Absolutely you can stay. Don't be silly." I lean down and kiss her to seal the deal.

Well, any lingering concern that Lainey living at my house would freak me out is completely quelled over the next couple of days. I end up feeling more connected to her than ever. I like playing house, but I want the real deal. I think about how I almost lost her, and how I have this strong urge to change my life.

Yeah, it's time to take this thing between us to the next level. What she and I had all along was good, I just couldn't see it. But now that I do, I want even more. Lainey is already in my heart, where it counts, but now I feel her in my bones, in my marrow. When I make love to her, I no longer know where I end and she begins. What we have needs to be made permanent.

That's why when, two nights later as I'm holding her in my arms, I ask for something I never thought I would. "Will you stay with me, Lainey?"

As she toys with a loose thread on my tee, she looks up and laughs. "I *am* staying with you, Nolan."

"I mean...more."

She shifts on the sofa, giving us some space. "Like, how much more?"

I lay it on the line then. "I'm asking you to not go to Chicago."

Looking away, she murmurs, "Are you sure you *really* want that?"

I blow out a breath, sit up and lean forward, elbows on my knees. This isn't going to be easy. Despite the great progress we've made the past few days, Lainey still doesn't fully trust me. Not that I blame her. I created this. And only I can fix it.

I start on fixing it now by reminding her, "You said yourself that love means more to you than any job ever will, right?"

"That's true," she confirms, nodding. "And I'd give up just about anything for you, Nolan. But I don't want to say no to the Chicago position, and have you regretting it later."

"Ah, I understand your concern, Lainey. But this time is different. I'm not going to change my mind, I promise. I want you, for now and for forever."

I can tell she wants to give in, but my stupid actions of the past have her understandably hesitant.

"I don't know," she hedges. "If I decline the offer, I'm right back to being jobless. And I sure as hell can't go back to work at the casino. Not after…" she trails off.

I urge her then to move closer to me. When she does, I sit up straighter and start rubbing her back, hoping to soothe her.

"Rest assured," I say softly. "I don't *ever* want you going back to the casino job."

Leaning back into my kneading hands, she asks, "What would I do, though?"

"The marketing job with the Wolves is still open," I remind her. "They haven't hired anyone yet."

"I heard that too," she says. "But that doesn't mean they plan on hiring me. Despite Brent, Aubrey, and you, Nolan"—she twists around and pins me with a knowing look—"lobbying hard for me, I haven't heard a word from them."

Okay, so now I know that she knows I put in a good word for her. But so did Brent and Aubrey. And it's due to one thing, something I share with her now.

"You know we all vouched for you because we know you'd kick ass in that job."

"Yeah, I would," she replies confidently.

Ah, there's the Lainey I know and love.

"So stay," I press once more.

She sits back next to me and, after a moment of contemplation spent chewing away at her bottom lip, she proclaims, "Well, I don't really *want* to live and work in Chicago."

"That sounds like a yes to me."

"It's a maybe, Nolan."

"What's holding you back?" I inquire.

"Well, for one, where would I live? No job means zero income. I can't stay with Brent and Aubrey forever, nor would I want to."

I reach over to tuck a loose strand of dark hair behind her ear. "You could always move in with me. Like, for good."

That makes her laugh...and laugh...and laugh. "And what?" she says at last. "Become your kept woman?"

Lainey's kidding around, but I'm sure as hell not when I then propose, like literally—"We could always go legit. You could become my wife."

That leaves her totally and utterly speechless, like I knew it would. "Bet you never saw that one coming," I murmur.

But when a full minute goes by and she hasn't uttered a peep, I start to worry.

"Uh, Lainey… Are you okay? You do know I'm serious, right?"

Still shell-shocked, she breathes out, "You really think we should get married?"

"That's generally what 'become my wife' would imply."

"So you're, like, for real proposing to me?"

"Yeah, I really am." We turn to one another, and I take her hands in mine. "I know this is all completely unconventional, but seriously"— my eyes meet hers—"I'm asking you to make me a happy man and marry me. I swear I'll spend the rest of my life trying to make you as happy as I feel right now."

"I am happy, Nolan," she says. "And I do love you…"

I see truth in her eyes that she loves me, but I still worry. Maybe she just doesn't want to marry me.

Shakily, I ask, "So what's your answer?"

"Well, we are kind of unconventional. But I just don't know…"

"Do you not want to marry me?" I dare to ask.

"It's not that."

What is it, then? Does she need a more formal proposal? I can do that.

Dropping to my knees, her hands still in mine, I look up and say, "I love you, Lainey Shelburne. Please…be my wife."

I still don't receive an answer, *but* I suspect one is coming.

I think it may even be a *yes*, seeing as she starts asking things like: "When would we do it? And where would it happen? Would we have a big wedding, or a small one? And…" She stops and peers down at our entwined hands. "Would I get a ring?"

I laugh, thrilled that she's actually considering committing to a work-in-progress like me.

I then assure her, "You get whatever you want, babe. We can have a huge ceremony, or something tiny. As to the when and the where, those are up to you too. And of course you get a ring."

"Wow," she marvels, smiling. "When you go all-in, Nolan, I have to say you go all-in."

I raise a brow. "Is that a yes, then?"

"It is," she confirms.

Just to be sure we're not signing up for a long-distance union, before I start celebrating, I make sure to ask, "Chicago's out then, right?"

She rolls her eyes. "Clearly, Nolan."

"I just needed to hear you say it, is all."

We celebrate then, me by kissing the crap out of her, and her by giggling and pretending to dodge me, but then giving in. "God, I love you," I tell her.

"I love you too."

When we come back down to earth, I wrap her up in my arms and we lean back in the cushions of the sofa. *Ah, this life together is going to be amazing.*

A few seconds later, when I chuckle a little, she wants to know, "What's so funny?"

"I was just thinking about something."

"Yes?"

"I was thinking that I may be an all-in kind of guy, but you're an all-or-nothing kind of girl."

"Is that good?"

"It's great." I have to breathe her in then, so I bury my face in her hair and allow us to be just us—me and Lainey—for a while.

Eventually, though, I have to ask her some particulars regarding the wedding, which I'm kind of hoping will happen sooner rather than later.

"What kind of wedding do you think you want?"

"Hmm…" She purses her lips, then says, "I don't think I want a big production. That just seems so…I don't know…all-consuming or whatever."

"How do you mean?"

"I've watched Aubrey the past couple of months, with her upcoming wedding, and that level of planning holds no interest for me." She reaches out and touches my face, rubbing lightly at my stubble. "I'd rather put that energy into our relationship," she murmurs.

I laugh. "I knew there was a reason why I wanted to marry you." Then, in a more serious tone, I say, "Can I make another proposal?"

"Why the hell not. You're sure full of them tonight."

"That's right. I'm all-in here"—I point to my chest—"remember?"

She smiles, and I go on. "We have home games this week, and only two at that. Why don't we get married sometime during the next couple of days?"

Now that I've asked and she's accepted, I can't wait to make her Mrs. Solvenson. I guess I'm as all-or-nothing as she is. That's what makes us so right.

Lainey is fully onboard with tying the knot right away, so we start planning. I share some info I have on a tiny chapel just outside of Las Vegas. "I think it may be perfect for us," I say.

"How so?" she asks.

"For starters, every time I've ever driven by I think about how it'd be a cool place to get married. I have to warn you though that it's kind of small and humble. But if that's what we want, something—"

"Intimate, but special," she finishes for me, and then proclaims,

"Then it'd be the right place."

"Exactly."

We laugh at how in-synch we are now, and lying back on the sofa, I take her with me.

Yeah, this is going to be perfect, our eyes say when our gazes meet. Being this close, I have to kiss her, which I do for a good, long while. Eventually, though, we get back to planning, seeing as the wedding is so soon.

"What about the invite list?" I proffer.

Lainey thinks it over, tapping a finger to her lips, plump from so much kissing.

"Well," she begins, slowly sitting up. "I obviously want Aubrey to be there. Our dream since we were little girls has always been to be each other's maid of honor."

I'm fine with that, of course.

Sitting up next to her, I say, "Brent should be my best man. And Benny and Dylan need to be there."

She nods in agreement. "I'd like to invite Eliza, as well."

We share a look, and then promptly lose it.

"Just don't throw her the bouquet," I say once we've recovered. "And I'll be sure not to toss Benny the garter. The last thing we need is to start our marriage with Coach T gunning for my balls."

"Hey!" She reaches over and cups said balls. *Shit, that feels good.* "No one guns for these except for me, especially after we're married."

The old me would've bristled over this show of possessiveness, but the new me welcomes it. There's no one I'd rather trust my balls to—or my heart, for that matter—than Lainey soon-to-be Solvenson.

32

THERE'S NO STOPPING US NOW

LAINEY

Nolan and I pick up our marriage license the next day. When we get in the car to leave the bureau office, I call the ad agency and give them the bad news that I won't be taking the position. Even without Nolan asking me to stay, I feel this is the best move for me. My heart was never in Chicago. I was simply trying to run away, and we all know how that works out. You simply take your problems with you.

"Are you ready to go see the chapel?" he asks when I finish the call.

"Yes." I smile over at him as I put my phone away. "Take me to church, Nolan."

He starts laughing, since the Hozier song of the same name—a tune we both love—comes on the radio at that exact second. He turns up the volume as he drives us out to the quaint little chapel he told me about.

"Oh my word, it *is* perfect," I gush out a short while later.

I'm stepping from the car and taking in a picturesque white frame chapel with a cute bell tower and a tall steeple.

Taking Nolan's hand, I say. "Let's go talk to the pastor."

To our delight, the pastor, a kindly old gentleman who looks like Colonel Sanders, agrees to marry us the next day.

"Are you sure this isn't moving too fast for you?" I ask Nolan when we're back in the car. I guess there's some part of me that fears he'll panic and back out.

But when he turns to me and replies, "Lainey, there's no such thing as moving too fast, not anymore. My love for you is no longer defined by time," I know he's in it for the long run.

"I love you so much, Nolan," I whisper in return.

He takes my hand, kisses the back. When he pauses, staring down at my fingers, looking aghast, I'm quick to ask, "Uh-oh. Is there a problem?"

"I'd say so! We need to get you a ring."

"Oh." I start giggling.

"Why are you laughing? This is serious business, lady."

I'm laughing since it's kind of amusing to see Nolan so invested. But there's no need to share that tidbit.

Composing myself, I reply, "I just never thought it would be a wedding ring that would have you so concerned. But you're right. We need to get a ring. Not just for me, but for you too."

We wait till we're back in the city to hit up a jewelry store. I go with a solitaire cut in platinum with little diamonds on the sides, and Nolan opts for a simple platinum band. We're having such a great time, but unfortunately my groom-to-be has to head home. He has a game tonight against the Blues and his routine, which cannot be altered lest it mess with the good hockey juju, requires him to take a nap and eat his usual game-day light snack.

Since there's still much more to do, I enlist Miss Wedding Planner herself, Aubrey, to go dress shopping with me. She's totally up for that, which is no longer the surprise it once would've been. Aubrey was a little shocked, of course, when I first informed her of this über-fast marriage. But when she saw how truly happy I am, she finally conceded that Nolan must be right for me.

So dress shopping it is.

The great thing about Vegas is that weddings are big business. Finding what I need is a snap. I not only pick out a dress that I love, but I choose flowers and a photographer, as well.

By five o'clock, we're done and back at Aubrey's.

"I just don't know how you do this wedding stuff day in and day out," I say to her as I flop down on her sofa and kick off my heeled sandals. "I'm whooped, and my whole body is achy."

Aubrey arches a brow. "You sure that achiness isn't from too much Nolan?"

"Oh my God, is that a sex joke?"

Aubrey looks sheepish as she sits down next to me. "I guess it is," she says, giggling.

I'm not surprised at the joke, as she and I are pretty open about sex. What I'm shocked over is she's teasing around about me having sex with *Nolan*.

"So you really don't hate him anymore," I quietly inquire. "You're not just onboard with this because of me?"

"Lainey, I never hated him."

"Okay, well, you disliked him profusely, then."

"Fair enough," she declares. "But I don't *dislike him profusely* anymore. And it's not just a new development because of the wedding. I was coming around even before, as you know."

"I did notice," I say, recalling the time she brought him up when I first mentioned moving to Chicago. "But I'd love to know what changed your mind?"

She smiles. "First of all, I could tell *he* was changing from some things Brent mentioned. And you were changing too, Lainey. But it's good that I have come around because I couldn't be hating on the man about to become my brother-in-law, right?"

"True," I agree. And then, because she's Aubs and I have to share good things with her, I say, "God, I really can't wait until tomorrow is finally here. After the ceremony, Nolan and I can start living our lives as husband and wife, forever and ever."

Aubrey's quiet then, so I ask, "You're still onboard, yeah?"

"Of course."

"What's wrong, then?"

"Nothing," she says on a sigh.

"Come on," I press, wondering what could possibly be bugging her after she seemed so fine with everything.

Finally, she tells me. "It's just, are you sure you're okay with such a rushed wedding? You know Mom and Dad are going to have a fit that you're doing this without them."

"I've actually thought about that," I confess. "But I think they'll be okay with it. You know me...and so do they. I've always been the unpredictable wild child, so this is kind of par for the course."

"It is," Aubrey agrees. And then, eyes widening, she says, "Oh my God. You're not pregnant, are you?"

I assure her I'm absolutely not, and she visibly relaxes. I try then to explain why I want to get married so quickly.

"It's not a bad reason," I say. "This is just how Nolan and I want things to be. At first, I thought it was just him, seeing as how once he's in, he's all-in. But then I realized I felt the same way. We're both like that. Hell, we have been from the start. We slept together within hours of meeting each other, Aubrey. And trust me, we were both very much all-in on that one too."

Eyes snapping to me, Aubrey points a finger my way. "I knew it!" she says. And then narrowing her eyes, she asks, "Did Brent know about you and Nolan? I'm asking only because he always used to act so shifty when I'd bring you guys up. Not so much anymore, but definitely early on."

With a sly smile, I finally admit, "He may have caught me coming in on New Year's morning."

"May have or did, Lainey."

First, I make sure she won't be pissed at Brent, and once she agrees, I admit, "He did. He caught me on a classic walk of shame."

Rolling her eyes, she says, "I doubt that. You're pretty much shameless, little sis. Like Nolan."

"And that, big sis, is why he and I are so perfect together."

She can't dispute that, not one little bit.

33

SPREADING THE LOVE

NOLAN

The game against St. Louis is a rout. We win big, 8-3, with me scoring two of the goals and assisting on a third.

"That was one hell of a game, Solvenson," Dylan says to me afterward when we're in the locker room.

I'm in my stall, waiting to be interviewed, and he's standing next to me. The press is still talking with Brent, but I'm up next.

Wiping the sweat from my forehead, I share the truth with my friend. "I was feeling extra motivated tonight."

Looking over at me pointedly, he replies, "Think maybe that has something to do with your secret plans for tomorrow?"

I can't help but break into a big, fat grin. "I think it does, my friend. I think it does."

Out of the players, only Brent, Benny, and Dylan, all of whom are invited to the ceremony tomorrow afternoon, are aware of my impending nuptials. I figure I'll share the news with the rest of the team afterward. If I let it slip ahead of time, especially here in the locker room, all the guys will show up at that tiny church out in the desert. And though a part of me would be totally fine with that, I want to keep this small and meaningful, like Lainey and I agreed.

The next day arrives, and it's time to make Lainey Shelburne my wife. I can't wait!

Brent, who happily agreed to be my best man, offers to drive me out to the church. Lainey is already there and has been since morning. She left with Aubrey and Eliza earlier so she could dress and get ready in one of the little back rooms at the chapel. This is all hearsay, however, since I haven't been allowed to see her.

"There will be no seeing the bride before the wedding," Lainey informed me last night when she refused to stay over at my house, which will be her house, as well, after today.

I told her as much, but she insisted, "Some traditions are worth preserving, Nolan. And this is one of them."

I left it at that.

"So you ready for this, man?" Brent asks, interrupting my reverie as we leave the city limits and drive out into the more desolate parts of the desert.

"Bro, I am more ready for this than you could even imagine."

Brent glances over at me. "That's a pretty strong statement from a man who was opposed to love and marriage until just recently."

"Yeah…" I blow out a breath. "I guess it took a Shelburne woman to make me finally see the light."

Brent chuckles. "That'll happen, my friend. That'll happen."

He would know.

We're quiet for a bit, till we come upon a small diner on the side of the road. It's the only thing for miles and the sign out front declares it as the *Area 51 Café.*

Brent slows down considerably, for some unknown reason.

Glancing over at the café, with an inexplicable huge grin on his face, he mutters, "Shit, I almost forgot."

"Forgot what?" I ask, perplexed.

He reaches under his seat and pulls out a rectangular box, one wrapped in crazy Day-Glo green paper.

Tossing it over to me, he says, "A little extra gift from me and Aubrey…for you and Lainey."

I shake the box, but can't figure out for the life of me what it could contain. Nor do I have the slightest idea why Brent's still smiling like a crazy man.

"What is it?" I flat-out ask. "And what's with the glow-y green paper." *An odd choice for a wedding gift, that's for sure.*

"Dude, it's a surprise. And you'll see soon enough that the paper fits the gift."

"Whatever that means," I mutter.

"Just open the gift tonight with Lainey. It'll all make sense then." He shoots me a smug grin. "And, Nolan, you can thank me later."

34

AREA 51 REVISITED

LAINEY

The chapel interior is absolutely stunning. There are flickering candles everywhere and beautiful flowers bestowing a fragrant aroma. Nolan and I couldn't have chosen a more suitable venue to commit ourselves to one another.

And so that is what we proceed to do—commit ourselves to one another, before God and the pastor, before Brent and Aubrey, and before Dylan, Eliza, and Benny.

"I love you," I murmur against Nolan's lips when he starts kissing me after we're declared husband and wife.

He says it back, and then deepens the kiss. Our friends whoop and holler.

"Save it for tonight," Benny yells out.

"You go, girl," Eliza chimes in.

The pastor just chuckles and lets us go to town. I could definitely kiss Nolan all day and into the night, but our friends are waiting.

Reluctantly, we break apart. "We'll continue this later," he promises, his sapphire eyes blazing with desire.

"Tonight," I murmur, "and into tomorrow too."

"For the rest of our lives," he amends, kissing me once more.

Ah, love...

The pastor turns us around then and introduces us as Mr. and Mrs. Solvenson. There's more cheering, and we take a bunch of pictures over the next hour. After we leave the chapel, our small group convenes for an amazing celebratory dinner at Aubrey and Brent's house. But it's when we return to Nolan's place—well, mine now too—that I begin to feel like we're really married.

That makes me so happy that I start to cry.

"Aw, baby." Nolan takes me in his arms. "You're not having second thoughts now, are you?"

"No, never." I lean my head against his strong shoulder. "I'm just so happy right now. I'm overwhelmed, but in a good way."

"I hear you, sweetheart," he whispers. "I feel exactly the same way."

And then he shows me that he does.

The first time we're together as man and wife, Nolan makes slow, sweet love to me.

The second time, it's more frenzied.

Afterward, as we're lying entangled in the sheets, I notice a gift we forgot to unwrap.

"Wonder what's in that one," I say to Nolan as I jerk my thumb toward the mystery present from Aubrey and Brent. "Though why they chose such an obnoxious green wrapping for a wedding gift is beyond me."

"It supposedly matches the gift in some way," he informs me. "But what I can't figure out is why passing a diner named after Area 51 made Brent suddenly remember the damn thing."

My eyes widen as I recall an *incident* Aubrey once told me about. It occurred back when she and Brent were first embarking on their relationship, back when it was strictly professional. Well, mostly.

I start giggling.

"What is it?" Nolan asks. "Do you know what's in the box?"

I start laughing so hard then that it takes me a full minute to recover. When I do catch my breath, I say, "Yes, I think I have an idea of what the gift could be."

"Okay, let's see if you're right." Nolan slips out of bed and pads over to the dresser to retrieve the present.

He's completely naked, so I watch with appreciation as his glutes tighten with each step. *Damn, that man's ass is beyond fine. And those wide shoulders, gah!* He turns to face me, and I look down. *Yeah, that part of him is pretty stunning, as well.*

He clears his throat, cocking a brow when he sees the lust-filled look I'm giving him. His *actual* cock goes up a little too. Just wait till he sees what's in the box.

"Open it," I purr as I lounge back in the tangled sheets invitingly.

He rips away the green paper.

"Area 51," he says out loud once the wrapping is on the floor. "What is this, some kind of toy?"

"Oh, it's a toy all right."

He starts smiling as he checks the packaging out more thoroughly.

"Ah," he says when he realizes what *kind* of toy it is.

He rips it open and takes out a florescent green vibrator. Holding it aloft, like some kind of funky-ass light saber, he flicks on a switch and says, "Check it out. It fucking glows."

"It's also supposed to have some sort of pulsating action," I chime in as I start to remember the details Aubrey shared with me. "That's one we ladies supposedly *really* like."

"It says here it actually has *vibrating* pulsating action," Nolan corrects as he scans the torn-away packaging, using the glowing vibrator for extra light.

"Ooh, even better," I say.

He tosses the packaging aside and flicks another switch on the toy. The green thing starts to wiggle like crazy and, as he holds it steady to turn off that movement feature, it starts glowing brighter.

"Oh yeah, I remember Aubrey saying it glows brighter and brighter as your body, um, warms it up."

Raising a brow, he looks over at me and asks, "Should we turn off that light feature, then? I do make you pretty hot, babe." *Cocky bastard, but he has good reason.* "You think it'll be too much?"

"No, wait." I glance over at a window that happens to face Brent and Aubrey's house and I'm struck with the best idea. Though we're a couple of houses apart, this second-floor room is high enough that the glow should go over the roofs and straight into Brent and Aubrey's place.

"Actually," I go on, my naughty idea blossoming. "I think we need to open the blinds a little more. That way, Brent and Aubrey will know for sure that we opened their gift. *And* that we're putting it to use."

Nolan laughs. "Hell, this thing is so bright I think the whole neighborhood will know something is up."

He's kidding...I think. But then again, the vibrator is rather blinding. In the end, we open the blinds only a crack. That way anyone, besides Aubrey and Brent, who notices the glow-y green coming from our room will probably just think we like to get busy in weird lighting.

But Aubrey and Brent will know the truth. They'll know we took a little trip to Area 51. Not the otherworldly location but, as I soon discover, a place where you certainly *feel* otherworldly.

35

COMING CLEAN

NOLAN

I decide to announce the news that Lainey Shelburne and I got hitched on the *Marty Quick Show*. Full circle and all that, seeing as it was when I was on Marty's show last summer that I finally realized I wanted—no, wait, I *needed*—Lainey back in my life. I wasn't where I needed to be at the time, but it was a first step.

To think I was so fucking worried that Marty had discovered I'd once been married, and that I had failed miserably at being someone's husband.

Now I don't care about any of that.

That's why this is unfinished business I intend to finish once and for all. That's right, there'll be no more secrets for me, and therefore no more worrying about shit coming back to bite me in the ass. This is the new me, living a new life, with my girl Lainey at my side. I've learned from the past, and I'm no longer intimidated, nor stifled, by it.

In other words, I got this shit by the balls.

The first week in December, we have a game against Toronto that's up in Toronto. That sets the wheels in motion. I'm due to fly in early with the team, so I schedule the interview with Marty to take place the day before the game.

But I'm not doing this alone, no way.

I secure permission from the powers-that-be to take Lainey with me on the team plane. Management knows we recently got married, and I've informed them of my plans to make the official announcement on Marty's show. They're okay with that, as they like good publicity, and this is certainly what my announcement will be.

The players finally know we tied the knot, which means the flight to Toronto is filled with champagne toasts and lots of good-natured ribbing.

"Best of luck to you both." Breeze, our goaltender, raises his glass from across the aisle.

I tap my flute to his, and Lainey, leaning over from the window seat, does the same.

Breeze then declares, "Gorka!"

"What's that mean?" Lainey wants to know.

"It a Russian toast, and mean you must now kiss," Breeze informs us with a clap.

"Hell, we can do that." I turn to Lainey and press my lips to hers. We then proceed to make out for a good solid minute.

But then someone from the back of the plane yells "get a room," and we break apart.

"I think there's gonna be some scoring once we land," I hear Benny say from where he's seated behind Breeze. "Someone's getting lucky today."

Dylan, from behind me, chimes in, "I bet we see a little Solvenson coming along soon, what with the way these two are all over each other all the time."

I start laughing.

"Jeez, Dylan," Lainey says as she twists around to address him over the top of the seat. "Give us a little time first to just enjoy being newlyweds. We'll think about kids later."

"Hey, that doesn't mean you can't practice a bunch," he retorts, chuckling.

"Oh, we plan on doing that," I mutter as I squeeze Lainey's leg high up on her thigh.

Humming happily, Lainey agrees. "Yeah, there'll be lots and lots of practice."

Brent, across the aisle and seated next to Breeze, groans. Leaning forward, he says, "Hey now, that's a little too much information for me, Future Sister-in-Law. Seeing that funky green glow coming from your bedroom window your wedding night was more than enough."

"Hey, *you* bought us the gift," Lainey volleys back.

Brent chuckles. "Yeah, you have a valid point."

And then he's full-on laughing when I murmur, "Best. Damn. Gift. Ever."

Brent reaches over Breeze to fist-bump me. "Dude," he says, giving me a knowing look.

"You were absolutely right about that one," I assure him in a low voice.

All the players around us then want to know what we're talking about. I change the subject by pouring more champagne for the guys. Some things, like your new wife's love of sex toys, need to stay sacred.

A while later, and after we land in Toronto, our great day continues. Once we're checked in the team hotel, Lainey receives a call from Mrs. Fielding, the director of marketing for the Wolves. She informs her that the entry-level marketing job Lainey interviewed for is hers if she wants it.

Of course, she accepts.

When Lainey is done with the call she turns to me, hands on her hips, and says, "Is this your doing, Mr. Solvenson?"

I inform her it's not, which is the truth. "You earned this on your own merits, Mrs. Solvenson."

"Wow," she muses, smiling. "I like how that sounds."

"Which part? The fact that you got the job on your own...or the fact I can now call you Mrs. Solvenson?"

"Both," she replies, "but I especially love the Mrs. Solvenson part."

"Yeah, me too."

I'm all set to show her just how much I love how her sharing my surname sounds, but then her mom calls, interrupting the fun. I leave Lainey be, giving her time to talk. Her parents were, understandably, a little upset we got married so quickly, and, of course, without them in attendance. But they understand how Lainey is, so they're coming around.

When Lainey finishes with the call, she informs me we'll be fully forgiven if we make her parents' house our destination for Christmas dinner. Since my big family will be fine without me hanging out with them on the actual holiday, I tell her to call her mom back and tell her we'll be there with bells on.

"Well, maybe not literally," she says.

"Why not?" I tease. "It is Christmas."

She throws a pillow at me, and calls her mom back. Her parents are thrilled. I'm glad that they're happy, but, more importantly, Lainey is smiling.

"Everything is turning out so well," I murmur in her hair as I wrap my arms around her.

She leans back against me. "It is, Nolan. Our new life is pretty darn close to perfect."

I can't disagree, and we're still flying high a couple of hours later when we arrive at Marty Quick's studio for the interview.

Once our headphones are in place, we're told we're almost set to broadcast. There's a commercial break first.

Marty, seated across from us, uses the time to look over his notes. Meanwhile, Lainey leans in to me and whispers, "Are you nervous at all?"

She knows I intend to set the record straight, not just regarding our recent nuptials, but also by revealing my past.

"Not really," I reply. "I actually feel really good that I'm doing this."

I do too. So much so that I kick off the interview by announcing rather early on that Lainey and I are now husband and wife.

"Wow," Marty replies, clearly astonished. "Does that mean you just gave me an exclusive?"

"Pretty much, Marty," I confirm with a smirk. "Only our family, friends, and my teammates know, so it looks like you did indeed just break the news."

Marty knows his ratings just shot through the roof. He smiles over at me, nodding in appreciation. He won't dare ask any hardball questions now, nor will he dig for any dirt. But it doesn't matter; there's nothing left to hide. Or rather, there won't be real soon.

First, however, we talk more about the wedding. Lainey shares some details about our small but perfect ceremony, which Marty eats up. But soon enough, he says to me, "So, Nolan, my producers informed me you have more to say on the subject of marriage."

"Yes." I nod somberly, and it's like you can hear a pin drop in the studio. "Marty, you may recall me acting a little cagey at our last meeting."

Marty's right on that one. "Regarding the strippers, eh?"

Lainey quietly interjects, "For the record, those days are over."

"Yes, they are," I confirm.

"Of course," Marty agrees, dropping the stripper angle.

I then say, "What I was worried you'd uncovered that day, Marty, was something virtually no one knows. You see, my marriage to Lainey"—I glance over at her, and she smiles at me encouragingly—"is not my first."

Our host drops his pen. "What? It's not?"

Seeing Marty Quick so utterly stunned is abso-fucking-lutely priceless. I continue, unprompted, sharing the tale of my first marriage and how it ended. I don't go into explicit detail. I simply state it was dissolved quickly due to infidelity.

"Not on my part," I hasten to add.

"Amazing that this never came out," Marty marvels.

"It was a long time ago," Lainey interjects.

"Yes, it was," Marty agrees. And then, turning to me, he says, "Still, I give you credit, man, for taking the plunge again."

"Ah," I softly reply. "We've reached the *real* reason why I'm here, beyond simply confessing my past to you."

"Wait, there's more?" Marty's practically frothing at the mouth, eager for dishing more dirt, but unfortunately for him my next words are simply a love letter to Lainey.

I go on to talk about how she made me face my demons from the past, and how I'm a better man for it. I gush about realizing what a gift it is to find love, and how I'm learning to embrace it.

"I was always resisting," I tell Marty, but also I'm telling Lainey, since she needs to hear this too. "I fought, and I fought. But I was only ever fighting myself. I was hurting *me*, holding back from who I could be."

"So who are you now?" Marty asks, seemingly genuinely interested to hear my reply.

So I give it to him.

"That's an easy one, Marty." I take Lainey's hand and face her, only her, as I tell the world, "I'm Nolan Solvenson, right winger for the Wolves and a Stanley Cup champion. But above all that, I'm Nolan Solvenson, Lainey Shelburne Solvenson's husband…and forever her man."

THE END

If you liked this story, please take a moment to leave a review. Even a short one means a lot.

Look for Benjamin "Benny" Perry's story, **Complications on Ice,** *set to drop like a puck in the summer of 2017!*

ABOUT THE AUTHOR

S.R. Grey is an Amazon Top 100 and a #1 Barnes & Noble Bestselling author. She is the author of the bestselling Boys of Winter hockey romance series, the popular Judge Me Not books, the Promises series, the Inevitability duology, A Harbour Falls Mystery trilogy, and the steamy Laid Bare series of novellas. Ms. Grey's works have appeared on multiple Amazon Bestseller lists, including Top 100 several times. She's also a #1 Bestselling Author on Barnes & Noble and a Top 100 Bestselling Author on iTunes.

S.R. Grey Facebook:
http://www.facebook.com/SRGrey

Author Website:
http://srgrey.com/

Sign up for S.R. Grey's exclusive-content newsletter and never miss an update, cover reveal, or release:
http://mad.ly/signups/106801/join

S.R. Grey on Twitter:
https://twitter.com/AuthorSRGrey

S.R. Grey Goodreads Author page:
http://www.goodreads.com/author/show/6433082.S_R_Grey

S.R. Grey on Instagram:

http://instagram.com/authorsrgrey#

S.R. Facebook Reading Group (join now for giveaways galore!):

https://www.facebook.com/groups/SRGreyHardAbsandHotBooks/

ACKNOWLEDGEMENTS

Thank you, first and foremost, to you—the readers! Big hockey hugs for everyone. And if you've read this far, please take a minute and leave a review for *Resistance on Ice*. Even a sentence or two of what you thought means the world.

Next, thanks to all the bloggers who help promote this series, as well as all my other novels. You are amazing and I couldn't do this without your help.

A big thank you to Christopher John for the cover photo and Najla Qamber for designing a book jacket that completely captures the feel of this book.

Also, thank you to Franci N., for taking another first look and giving me valuable feedback on Nolan and Lainey and the rest of the crew.

Thank you to Kristin S. and the amazing editing team over at Hot Tree Editing. And thanks to Emily and her team at E.M. Tippetts for formatting services that go above and beyond.

Last, but not least, thank you to my family and friends and my esteemed hockey "consultants." Y'all make this journey possible.

If you haven't already, here's your chance to read the first chapter of **Destiny on Ice**, Brent Oliver's story, and the first novel in the *Boys of Winter* series. Oh, and there's some Nolan in there too.

GOLDEN BOY GETS A LITTLE TARNISHED

BRENT

My father was a great hockey player. Back in the day, in the era of eighties' big hair and synthesized music, Billy Oliver won not just one, but two Stanley Cups. He was awarded the Conn Smythe trophy both times and has received an assortment of other hardware throughout the years.

He's retired now, but my dad was once a star.

To me, though, he's always just been Dad.

But as his only child, I have a legacy to live up to. I pray I don't disappoint him. I pray someday I'll be as good as he once was. And damn it, I better win a freaking Stanley Cup like he did.

I have no choice, not really. Since the moment my father first laced up hockey skates on my three-year-old little feet, the look of pride on his face told me even then all I needed to know—anything short of being the best will never do.

And guess what?

In many ways, I've become the best at what I do, which is, like my dad, play professional hockey.

I've been good since the start, a natural some say. I don't know about that, but I do know that even before I was drafted—in the first round by the Las Vegas Wolves, an expansion team at the time—I was being called "The Golden Boy" and "The Next One."

These days, three years later, I'm pretty much the poster boy for the NHL. And I have a slew of endorsement deals to prove it.

Lately, though, I've been falling short.

And I really don't know why.

Something is missing for me in the game. Or is it something that's missing in *me*?

I blow out a breath and shake my head.

Things started out so great. Where'd it all go wrong?

I made a name for myself early on. Expansion teams usually struggle for years before posting a winning record. Not so for the Wolves. With me centering what was then a subpar line, I was still able to make us shine. We came out swinging that first season in the league.

BRENT OLIVER SCORES THE GAME-WINNING GOAL IN HIS AND THE WOLVES' FIRST NHL GAME, SETS UP TEAMMATES FOR TWO MORE

One month later, there was this:

THE WOLVES OFF TO A COMPLETELY UNEXPECTED STELLAR START

Then things started to slide.

Those subpar players on my line weren't enough to keep afloat a pretty much overall crappy team, even with me centering. The Wolves' owners and management made the necessary moves—they don't mess around when shit needs to get done.

We picked up a phenomenal winger, Nolan Solvenson. He started to play and things turned around.

ADDING SKILLED RIGHT-WINGER NOLAN SOLVENSON TO ROOKIE BRENT OLIVER'S FIRST LINE PROVING TO BE A MASTERFUL MOVE

ON A MID-SEASON WINNING STREAK, THAT SOLVENSON TRADE IS PAYING OFF FOR THE WOLVES!

Another trade made at the deadline gave us Benjamin Perry. A big, strong left-handed winger, he was the final piece to the puzzle. Even with far-from-elite second, third, and fourth lines, it didn't matter. Not with me, Benjamin, and Nolan on the first line. We could *not* be stopped.

Benjamin—or Benny, as he's known to the team—is adept at using his size and muscle to check the hell out of any sorry soul who happens to be matched up against him. He simply wears other players down… and then it's a fucking scorefest. Thanks, in part, to his killer slapshot.

Together with Nolan, a sniper in his own right, we were—and in many ways still are—quite a force to be reckoned with. We destroy teams, though not as much lately. But back then, man, we were racking up so many points that the press branded us the OPS line, as in Special Forces.

THE OPS LINE'S SNIPERS OF OLIVER, PERRY, AND SOLVENSON ELIMINATE THE COMPETITION WITH EASE

THERE'S NOTHING COVERT ABOUT THIS LINE'S SCORING PROWESS

We worked our reputation to our advantage. Trash-talking on the ice and taunting players became our pastimes. We also happened to get a lot of pucks in the net.

Ah, the good old days.

We still trash-talk and taunt, but we aren't as lethal as we once were.

"We just need to get back on track," I murmur to myself. "The season doesn't start for a few more weeks. I'll have my shit together by then."

I better, since I'm the captain of the team. If I go down, we all sink. And that's not fair to anyone, especially not to my linemates, Nolan and Benny. Over the past couple of years they've become my best friends, which is a blessing and a curse. It's a blessing that we play so well together, but it's a curse that we also have a tendency to fuel each other's vices.

God knows this off-season we've become far too focused on partying and women. Like me, my linemates are extremely popular. Hell, let's not mince words—we're gods. In the hockey world, it's good to be a god. Guys want to *be* you and girls want to *do* you. Multiply that all by a hundred if you're not an ogre in the looks department.

And none of us are.

Not to brag—though, I guess I kind of am—but I have the most women falling at my feet. Hell, I've had women who've wanted to *lick* my feet.

Like, literally.

There was this crazy bitch this one time…

Wait, I digress. Back to where our team is today—floundering in a sea of mediocrity.

After that first good regular season, we fell apart during the playoffs. A dirty hit that sent me flying into the boards also sidelined me with a concussion. It didn't end there. More bad luck plagued our team. Nolan went into a scoring slump, and Benny took a punishing check against the boards that broke his foot. We were knocked out of the playoffs in the first round.

I went to Minneapolis, my hometown, to sulk.

"Next year will be different," my always-positive father tried to reassure me.

He was wrong.

We missed the playoffs entirely the following year, for reasons still unknown.

Then there was the season that just ended this past spring—another disappointment.

LAS VEGAS WOLVES FOLD, KNOCKED OUT ONCE AGAIN IN THE FIRST ROUND

Needing a break from all things desert-life, I said to Nolan and Benny, "Fuck this shit."

That was over three months ago. We were in the middle of cleaning out our lockers for the summer. My linemates looked at me, confused.

And then Nolan finally asked, "Fuck what shit, Oliver? What are you going on about over there?"

"Everything," I replied, gesturing around the empty locker room. "We're done, finished. Let's get the hell out of this place for a while."

I meant Las Vegas the city—and I think Nolan was catching my drift—but Benny misunderstood.

"Dude," Benny began, "we *better* get outta here soon." He checked his watch. "We have a tee time at two."

He meant the golf game we had planned, but I was having none of that.

"Fuck golfing," I snapped. "I'm talking about *really* getting out of here. I think we deserve a much-needed break from this whole damn town."

Nolan looked intrigued. "What'd you have in mind?"

I happily shared with him and Benny what I'd been thinking about for days. "Let's head up to my house in Minnesota. We can spend the summer on the lake." I grinned, bad intentions in mind. "You know I'm a fucking rock star up there. We can party every night. Hell, we can fuck and get fucked up till training camp starts up in September."

Benny was in immediately, but Nolan had to think it over in his thoughtful kind of way.

At last, he said, "Okay, let's do it."

Since that day we've been partying like rock stars. Or, more accurately, like out-of-control hockey players.

We're still on a roll, even though it's August and we have to fly back to Vegas real soon. Until then, however, I've vowed my cool contemporary house by the lake will remain *the* place to party. It's our OPS base for debauchery, after all.

In reality, though, this craziness can't go on. We all know that.

Even wild and crazy Benny had the sense to ask me just last week, "Dude, what should we do?"

"About what?"

I was in the midst of texting a local puck bunny to see if she wanted to meet me for a quickie, so I was a bit distracted.

Benny sighed. "We gotta report to camp in a less than a month. Guess it's time to start thinking about slowing down with the girls, the booze, the—"

I put down my phone and cut him off with a raucous, "Hell no, my friend. We just need to scale it back a little."

"Scale it back in what way?" Nolan, who walked in the room just at that moment, wanted to know.

I shrugged. "Maybe have smaller parties? Maybe drink a little less?"

We all agreed to those things, but we haven't followed through. In the past seven days we've abstained from partying for all of two.

This is so not going to play well with the team. My diet is crap, and I'm nowhere near peak playing shape. Sure, my body looks all lean and cut, meaning you'd never know I wasn't ready to hit the ice rearing to go, but looks can be deceiving. I went out for a run just the other day and came back fucking winded as hell.

That was a first.

Still, I'm confident I can get back into playing shape in no time. It's the inside of my head that's kind of a mess. I just don't fucking care about winning, not anymore. I mean, I do, but I don't. Does that make sense?

Nah, it doesn't to me, either. But I better figure it out, and fast.

Where's my drive to get my shit together? Where's my commitment to winning, my obligation to my players?

I ask myself these things every day now, but I guess the answers are clouded by my drinking copious amounts of alcohol and fucking way too many puck bunnies.

Dad would be so proud—not.

Well, he would be glad I diligently use protection. I haven't gone *that* far off the rails. Still, wrapping my dick up isn't enough to keep management off my ass. My agent already informed me—this morning, in fact—that the Wolves' ownership group has a pretty good idea of what I've been up to, along with my teammates, here in Minneapolis.

I listened half-heartedly when my agent woke me up to say, "Don't blow this off, Brent. Management is *not* happy with you. There's a certain image they expect you to uphold, and you're not doing that."

God forbid I'm not the team's "Golden Boy." I'm "The Next One," remember?

Bullshit, it's all crap.

Coach Townsend called me shortly after I got off the phone with my agent. He had the same warning.

"You don't want the team to take action. You're not going to like what they have in store for you, Brent, if you keep up with this bad behavior."

"Oh, come on," I replied, laughing. "The Wolves can't fire me. And what could be worse than that?"

Coach T chuckled like he knew something.

Hmm…

"I can't worry about that shit today," I said to him. "I'll start cleaning up my act tomorrow."

"Brent…" Coach T sounded doubtful.

"Really, I will," I insisted.

That was a few hours ago. And I plan to make some changes. But maybe not quite yet.

"Before tomorrow gets here," I justify to myself, "we still have the rest of today. And that means there's time for one more party."

I stride into the second-floor living room of my house, a spacious and angled space overlooking the huge lake on my property. Peering out at the crystal blue water, I announce to Benny and Nolan, "Listen up, boys. We're having one final blowout tonight, a party to end all parties."

There's a murmur from Nolan, but nothing from Benny.

"We're going to do this one right," I go on. "We party tonight. But then, when tomorrow arrives, we're done with messing around. We start training full-on."

Yeah, right, a little voice in my head coughs out.

I look around since no one besides my guilty conscience seems to be chiming in.

It's early afternoon and the sun is bathing the room—my favorite, by the way, with the way it juts out over the lake showcasing the floor-to-ceiling windows on two sides and a massive deck with a mile-long view on the other—in a warm summer glow.

Nolan, who is lounging on an easy chair with a beer in his hand, raises his bottle. "I'm in," he says.

His words aren't the least bit slurred, even though he's been drinking straight through since last night's bash.

"And then, yeah," he continues, agreeing with me, "we'll start getting ready for camp."

Despite his ability to suck down alcohol like a fish, Nolan hasn't veered too far off course. Getting back on track won't be hard for him. He's like Mr. Discipline. And he's not fooling anyone, anyway. I caught him working out in my basement gym a few days ago. With the way he was pumping iron I suspect he's been training consistently for a few weeks now.

There's still not been a response from Benny, which is unusual. Dude's always up for a party. He's probably the worst of us when it comes to out-of-control antics.

And that's saying a lot.

"Hey, where's Benny?" I ask Nolan as I scan the shadows of the room.

He nods to a sofa that's been pushed way-ass off to a far corner.

"Oh, I should've known." I chuckle as I take in an eyeful.

Benny is sprawled out on a sofa in the shadows, sleeping like a baby. His massive chest is rising and falling in perfect rhythm with the ticking clock on the stone mantel above his head. Some puck bunny he was fucking around with last night is with him, passed out on top of him.

The sheet covering their naked bodies is hiked up just enough to afford a view of the girl's creamy thigh, which is casually slung over my linemate's muscular, hairy-as-hell leg, and positioned under his semi-exposed junk.

Chuckling at Benny's total lack of modesty, I pick up a throw pillow and lob it at his head—the one that clearly controls all his thinking.

And he scores!

As the pillow makes contact—and how could it not with a pole like that marking my target?—the sheet falls off completely. I get a quick flash of perky tits and tiny ass. And then, shit—a big honking piece of man-meat assaults my eyes.

"Dude," I snort, mock-offended. "You need to cover that shit before you blind us all."

Benny stirs to life. Sitting up, he barks, "What the fuck, Oliver? I was having the best dream ever. That is till you started tossing shit at my balls. "

Nolan lets out a low chuckle. "Only you, Benny, could find a way of using 'tossing' and 'balls' in the same sentence. But really"—he tilts his bottle to Benny's dick—"you need to do what Brent said and cover that shit up."

Throughout this entire brain-draining exchange, the girl wakes up. And damn, she looks young. Letting out a little squeak, not unlike a hamster, she gathers the sheet around her naked self and scurries off to where she seems to think the bathroom is.

I only know this 'cause she's muttering something about having to pee. But the poor girl has no idea where to go. Hamster-girl flies past me, heading down the wrong hallway, the one that leads to my bedroom.

As I rush to retrieve her, I can't help but grumble, "Why in the hell do they always think the damn bathroom's down *my* hall?"

I catch up to and redirect the girl, pointing her in the correct direction. "It's that way, sweetheart," I say in my kindest tone.

No need to be an asshole; the poor thing already looks shell-shocked. Though whether that's due to waking up in a strange house or waking up next to that monstrous thing Benny calls a cock, I have no clue.

"Thanks, Mr. Oliver," she replies.

And then she runs off.

"*Mr.* Oliver?" I shake my head. "What the fuck is up with that? If she thinks I'm old and I'm only twenty-two, then…"

Whoa, wait.

Hurrying back out to the living room and pointing an accusatory finger at Benny, I say, "That chick better be over eighteen, dude. We're in enough trouble already with the team."

Benjamin Perry is twenty-eight, but he likes younger girls. Nothing illegal, so don't get your panties in a bunch. He just happens to favor babes who either look young, or are *just* old enough.

"She's twenty-three," he replies, sounding hurt by my accusation.

"What? Five years past eighteen?" Nolan peers over at me and smirks. "Hey, Oliver, you think Benny is working up to go cougar on us?"

Laughing, I reply, "Seeing as he's on his way to fucking the full spectrum of girls in their twenties, I do indeed think he's secretly working his way up to thirty."

"Small steps," Nolan says.

"Fuck you," Benny interjects. "You're both dickheads."

I put up my hands. "Hey, don't be pissed at me. Take it up with Nolan. He started with the jokes. I only brought up the chick's age for your own protection. I'm always looking out for you, buddy."

"Yeah, you usually are," he concedes. "And thanks for that." He shoots me an apologetic grin. "You really are a good kid at heart."

I shrug, feeling a little self-conscious at being called a kid. But then I see what Benny is up to, preparing to bust my balls.

Sure enough, the next words out of his mouth are "You do know I mean *kid* in a good kind of way. Like maybe"—he smirks—"a *golden boy* sort of style."

"Ha. Ha," I retort. And since he's enjoying yanking my chain far too much, I shoot him the bird. "Shut the fuck up, man."

Benny may give me a hard time, but his underlying sentiment is genuine. What he said about me being a good guy, like a decent person, is true. Despite all the craziness of late, I want nothing but the best for my friends. And just because I've been fucking up my own life lately doesn't mean Benny's and Nolan's lives have to go down the shitter too.

Really, I probably should've never invited them to Minnesota. I should have come up to the lake house by myself. That would've been the smart thing to do, especially if my intention all along has been to piss away my career.

I don't really want that, though, do I?

No.

I just need some help in getting back on track.

But where would I find something like that?

Ah, fuck it.

"So what do you say, Benny?" I ask, back to focusing on the party. "You in?"

He stretches, covering his dick with the pillow I threw at him. I make a mental note to have all my furniture *and* their decorative accents, especially the pillows, steam cleaned.

Running his hand through his shaggy, dark blond hair, he says, "Am I in for what?"

"Party tonight," Nolan interjects in his usual no-nonsense tone. "One last blowout, and then Brent here says we're stopping with the bad behavior."

I have to laugh. Nolan is only three years older than me, but it's like he's twenty-five going on forty. He's the voice of reason in our crew.

Well, most of the time.

Not today, though. No, today he agrees to go all-out.

With the party plans full steam ahead, we get on our phones, texting and calling everyone we know.

"Tonight we party hard," I declare when we reconvene in the living room.

"Yeah," Nolan says, holding up a freshly opened bottle of beer.

"You mean hell, yeah," Benny corrects, raising the full shot glass in his hand.

"Hell, yeah," I echo, a beer *and* a shot on the table in front of me. "And just so we're clear," I add. "Tomorrow we give up the booze and the women. Tomorrow we start training for real."

The boys agree, and we drink to our plan.

Yeah, tomorrow we'll do all those things…